FUSION

Contributors:
Stuart Aken, Danuta Reah, Katy Huth Jones,
Denise Hayes, Leonie Ewing, John Hoggard, Drew Wagar, Polly
Robinson, Jonny Rowland, David K. Paterson,
Thomas Pitts, Natalie Kleinman, Dawn Hudd, Peter Ford, Walt
Pilcher, John-Paul Cleary, Peter Holz, Apeksha Harsh, Brad
Greenwood, Joanna Vandenbring, Sarah Cuming
and Celia Coyne.

Published by Fantastic Books Publishing

FIRST EDITION

ISBN: 978-1500961879

© Copyright 2012 Fantastic Books Publishing

Cover art by B.Dziok
Cover design by Gabi Grubb

License Notes

This book is licensed for your personal enjoyment only.
This book in whole or part may not be reproduced or
copied without the written permission of the publisher.
Thank you for respecting the hard work of these authors and artists.

Introduction

Welcome to the Fantasy/Sci-Fi Fantastic Books International Charity Short Story Competition winners' anthology 2012. Potentially one of the longest book titles on the market, which is why we simply called it FUSION.

Included are the winning entries, the runners up, a few lucky last minute additions and two wonderful stories by our professional contributors Danuta Reah and Stuart Aken.

Don't forget to read the short biographies of our talented contributors.

Each story has been beautifully illustrated by digital artist Alice Taylor.

We hope you enjoy this anthology and will recommend it to your friends.

10% of the paid entry for the competition, plus 10% of the ongoing sales of this book will be donated directly to the WCRF (World Cancer Research Fund - Reg. Ch. No. 1000739) who do sterling work in the field of global cancer prevention.

Thank you for purchasing this book, you have contributed to an ongoing donation and your help is greatly appreciated.

Dedication

Ann Humphry (1955-2012)

We dedicate this anthology to the memory of Ann, a close family friend who lost her life to cancer just days before this book was released.

CONTENTS

Tam and the Giantess by Katy Huth Jones - 1

Bar-Code by Denise Hayes - 9

Infinite Maze by Leonie Ewing - 17

The Trouble With Dragons by Danuta Reah - 25

Baby Babble by John Hoggard - 37

Metal by Drew Wagar - 45

Dust to Dust by Polly Robinson - 51

The Flight of the Magician by Jonny Rowland - 59

The Changeling by Polly Robinson - 67

White Noise by David K. Paterson - 73

Other Things by Thomas Pitts - 79

Beyond the fringe by Natalie Kleinman - 89

Dorothy by Dawn Hudd - 97

Human Fossil by Denise Hayes - 105

Golf Planet by Peter Ford - 111

The Meeting at the Centre of the Universe by Walt Pilcher - 119

Afternoon Express by John-Paul Cleary - 125

The Removal Man by David K. Paterson - 131

Cat's Eye by Peter Holz - 137

Night Watch by Apeksha Harsh - 141

The Monkey's Kiss by Brad Greenwood - 147

The Warrior Woman by Joanna Vandenbring - 153

The Star Worker by Sarah Cuming - 165

The Truest Black by Celia Coyne - 171

Rebirth by Stuart Aken - 177

Tam and the Giantess by Katy Huth Jones

Tamika rubbed her saddle-sore bottom while a servant unfolded a red satin chair and placed it in the shade of a flowering tree. She perched on the seat and admired how the setting sun coloured the river in the valley below.

She glanced up at her bodyguard, Nagendra, looming above her like a second tree. 'I wish I could be a normal girl. A peasant, or a tradeswoman. Or even like you.'

'Normal?' Nagendra grunted. 'I wouldn't be calling me normal, m'lady.'

Tamika arched her back until she heard a pop. 'Oh, but you are. You won't have to be responsible for an entire duchy for the rest of your life.'

'Being responsible for you is as much as I dare put upon myself.' The giantess grinned. Her teeth, filed to points, dazzled white against her dark skin.

Tamika's smile faded. She made sure the servants could not overhear. 'What if I fail them? How can I rule Khala Rissala half so well as my father did?'

'M'lady. Tam.' Nagendra went down on one knee so she could lean closer. 'Your father said the same to me just before his coronation. And he was only a little older than you are. Only the arrogant or the fool will not admit to fear and doubt before accepting such a burden.'

Tamika grasped one giant hand between her two small ones. 'Promise me…'

Nagendra closed the other hand in a fist and held it over her heart. 'Anything, m'lady.'

'Promise you will never leave me.'

Nagendra chuckled. 'My life span should continue until your grandchildren's time. Unless…'

'Unless what?'

'Unless you wear me out with your worry!'

The tents were ready. Tamika entered the largest and gazed longingly at the camp bed. Nearly as large as her canopy bed at home, the furs had been pulled back from the feather pillow. The only thing missing was the usual basket of fruit, forbidden during her pre-coronation fast.

'I feel transparent,' whispered Tam. 'Are you sure you can't see through me?'

Nagendra chuckled. 'It's only the fasting. One more day, then the coronation, and then you will eat again.'

Tam sighed. 'Ah, food.' She sank cross-legged to the floor of the tent.

'Here, m'lady.' Nagendra gently lifted Tam and helped her stand again. 'Let's begin the meditation. It will help you forget your stomach.'

Tamika nodded and closed her eyes. She breathed deeply, exhaled loudly, brought her palms together.

'Let yourself be one with the earth power,' Nagendra intoned. 'Root yourself to its ancient foundations. Let your spirit soar, free from the boundaries of your body.'

Tamika opened herself to the pulsing energy that beat in time with her heart. It grew hotter and whiter as it poured into her.

For a moment she kept her thoughts outside the pillar of energy, questing beyond the camp, beyond the boundaries of time. But when the fire touched her bones, Tamika recoiled with a gasp. An image flashed in her mind of melting bones, charred flesh, agonized screams.

The light died, leaving her limp. No longer able to hold herself up, she fell into Nagendra's strong arms.

With a sigh, the giantess lifted Tamika to the bed.

'You came very close, m'lady.'

Tamika heard the disappointment in her voice. 'I'm sorry. It was so strong, it frightened me.'

'Did you see anything before you pulled away?'

Tamika shook her head. Had there been something, just before she panicked? She closed her eyes.

Dark is light, and light is dark. Shattered peace, like shards of glass dripping with blood....

Her eyes flew open and focused on Nagendra's worried face. 'I saw torches in the night. I heard the whistle of arrows in flight, and screaming.' She felt the blood drain from her face. 'We were attacked, or will be tonight.' She gripped Nagendra's hand, let a wave of nausea pass. 'Quickly, alert the guards.'

The giantess stood and brought her fist to her heart in salute. 'I had already doubled the watch, but I shall make certain they are prepared.' Before she left the tent, she looked back. 'There are many enemies of Khala Rissala who would gladly attack us before we reach the safety of the king's lands.'

Tamika curled on her side. She shut her eyes and felt herself spinning, swirling in a fog that clouded her thoughts. She heard Nagendra return but did not open her eyes.

'All is quiet for now, m'lady Tam.' Nagendra placed her massive hand on the pillow above Tamika's head. With gentleness, Nagendra crooned a lullaby that sent Tamika beyond the dizziness into a troubled sleep.

Tamika woke with a start. A throbbing like drums pulsed in time with her heartbeat. She slid off the bed, lurched to the entrance of the tent. Nagendra was already rushing about, waking everyone, giving orders.

Glimpses of light danced like fireflies in the night. A thin whistle in the air changed pitch as it approached her. An arrow smacked into the tent a handspan from her face. Tamika jumped. Her hands began to shake. Her feet would not move.

Attacked! Just like in her vision. What should she do? What would her father have done?

More arrows rained from the sky. A high-pitched ululation filled the air. As Nagendra turned, her body jerked. The giantess roared and fell to her knees, clutching her head. An arrow protruded from her eye. Tamika stared as the giantess's hands went limp and she slumped to the ground.

'No!' she screamed. Her eyes grew hot with tears, but she shut away the sight of her dear friend lying there, dead or dying. She gathered her despair and brought her trembling hands together.

Ignoring the screams and whistling arrows Tamika used her raw fear and rage to call up the earth power and root herself in it. When the hot white light filled her, she pushed past the pain, embraced it. With a shout that was part agony, part desperation, Tamika gathered a handful of fire, shaped it into a sphere, and flung the swirling energy into the air where it swelled and then burst in a shower of sparks.

When she sensed the enemy falter, she opened herself completely to the light and channelled it over the camp in a shield of living colours that hummed louder as they expanded. The sounds of attack changed to panicked retreat, but Tamika did not let go until she was certain the enemy was gone and would not return.

She wilted at the sudden loss of energy, but a surge of anguish gave her strength to go to Nagendra. The giantess lay on her side in a pool of her own blood.

Tamika moaned and fell to her knees when she saw the arrow protruding from Nagendra's eye socket. How could Nagendra be gone? What would she do without her? Tamika's vision blurred. She laid her small hand upon the blood-slicked neck.

Unbelievably she felt a pulse. She was alive! But just barely.

Without pause, Tamika sucked in a deep breath, again summoned the light. She cradled the great head in her hands and willed healing power to flow between them. Holding onto Nagendra's fading life force, Tamika wrenched out the arrow with the remains of Nagendra's eyeball. As she staunched the flow of blood, she brought the giantess out of her shock.

Nagendra moaned but did not open her remaining eye. Tamika used the energy to take Nagendra's pain as her own, and she cried out as she felt the stabbing, throbbing spike of agony in her own eye socket. She fought the instinct to recoil from it and cradled the pain instead until the feeling ebbed and finally vanished.

At last Tamika could focus on Nagendra's shallow breathing and erratic heartbeat. Using the power of the light, Tamika inhaled slowly and deeply and then audibly exhaled. She did this several times until Nagendra matched her breath for breath. By then her friend's great heart had returned to a strong, steady beat. With a sigh Tamika let the power fade and her strength with it.

Nagendra opened her eye to fix on Tamika. After a moment she grinned, flashing her pointed teeth.

'M'lady,' she whispered. 'Do you realize what this means?'

Tamika nodded, too overcome to speak.

Nagendra pulled herself to a sitting position, brought her hand to her ruined eye. 'Not only are you your father's daughter, but Tam, now I will look especially ferocious at your coronation.'

Tamika could only laugh as she threw her arms around Nagendra's neck. 'I don't care how frightening you appear to others, you will always be beautiful to me.'

They helped each other stand and called for a servant. Though he and Nagendra fussed over Tamika, she refused to sleep until she knew everything. Few had been injured, and none had wounds as grave as Nagendra's.

'Now we must both sleep for what remains of the night, for shortly we arrive at the city of the king, and the following morning you will be crowned.'

'And finally, I shall get to eat.' Tam's belly growled.

Nagendra chuckled while Tamika sank into the feather pillow. As she relaxed, the light enveloped her, comforted her, and she found the dreamless sleep of peace.

About the author: In addition to writing fantasy and science fiction since the age of eight, Katy Huth Jones plays piccolo and flute in a symphony, sews historic costumes, and loves unusual pets. She is a cancer survivor living with her husband Keith in the beautiful Texas Hill Country.

Website: www.katyhuthjones.com

Facebook: Katy Huth Jones

Twitter: @KatyHuthJones

Bar-Code by Denise Hayes

I can tell by the glint in her left eye that the Light Blue by the bar is interested. Sensory reactions in relevant regions of my anatomy suggest that the attract-signal in my own eye has been activated too. It's possible to short-circuit the trigger effect but I feel like some company tonight.

We find a room in a nearby encounter-block. The entry doorpad scans the bar-code on our palms and we're in. As transitory rooms go it's okay. The infobox shows radiation levels are low. An anti-bacterial cleanse took place only six hours ago.

The Light Blue smiles at one of the wall vodcams and slowly removes her clothes. Her languorous progress adds a beguiling old-style touch that is cosily erotic. She whispers 'Lights low,' but before the dimming is complete I say, 'No. Half-light.'

It'd be a shame not to appreciate the work that's gone into her. I'd guess that her breasts are by Cassandra Cross at Larolle; elaborate aureole patterns around perfectly symmetrical nipples. Her taut stomach is as white as crack with no tell-tale speckles of radiation damage. An exquisite accomplishment. Time to look closer.

I undress quickly. My own body is somewhat cut-price. It does, however, come into its own in action. First we check each other out. We press our bar-codes together and she emits a soft gasp. My own response is entirely internal. An electric ripple through my body. I close my eyes and read the print-out against my eyelids.

She's from the North and works in transportation. She enjoys role-play. Her left earlobe is a prime erotic zone. She's had 30 partners. Her last encounter was 24 hours ago with a Purple who recorded clear from any transferable diseases. She enjoys partners across the age spectrum (barring whites).

I'm happy with this and judging by the intense gleam in her eye she likes my info too.

But she's still concentrating more on the vodcam opposite than on me.

I press my off-the-peg breasts against hers, put my lips to her left ear and in a whisper too low to be picked up by any microphone say, 'Forget Big Brother, darling. Let's play Scissor Sisters'.

A few hours later I'm back in my static working on my database. I've never met my subject but it's impossible not to feel some affinity. I know him so well. It's perhaps just as well that the contact taboo keeps us at a distance.

Bard's led quite a life despite only being Dark Blue. He spent two years in the Mining Zone and by the time he came to me he'd been promoted to a terrestrial role in management. This gives him some financial clout that gains him entry into better-class bars, so data-basing him gives me a vicarious taste of the high-life.

Not that he isn't into a bit of lower-level surfing. The vodcam data shows he acquired his last partner in a cruising area. She was only a Pink and her barcode exchange recorded her as a maintenance worker. She'd had no work done and looked like a boy when stripped to the skin. Bard was rough with her and called her some disturbing names. I'm finding it hard, my fingers poised at my old-style keyboard, to know what to enter. I have to be truthful. There could be a spot-check and the camera, as they say, never lies. But there are ways of putting things. Stylistic options. If you take pride in your work and your subject, which I do, it's important to get it right.

His last sexual encounter was with a Pink. She checked clear of transferable diseases. They engaged in imaginative experimentation. He requested a further meeting. She declined.

I order ENTER and close down for the night. I'll catch up with Bard tomorrow.

A few days later I see the Light Blue again in the same bar. She's glinting away at me but she's out of luck. I feel in the mood for a bit of hetero-vanilla tonight. I'm considering moving to another bar when a drink appears on the counter in front of me.

'Couldn't catch your eye so I thought I'd take a direct approach.'

It's a rough-hewn Dark Blue with black curls and hazel eyes (with no glint at all). He's strongly built unlike most men in my social group who tend to be pale and attenuated as if they've spent too long in the dark.

I feel an electric tingle in my eye, though I'm getting no such signals from him.

I frown. 'You all talk?'

'Not really. Just switched-off.'

'Ah, okay. Let's go.'

'Shall we finish our drinks first?' He grins and I smile. This promises to be an interesting session.

We take a Black-Train to his static. The blinded windows preserve geographical anonymity. It's best to keep life simple.

When we arrive I'm disappointed by the run-down nature of his accommodation.

The night air is noxious. I'm unused to external sites and my throat itches. The Dark Blue is fiddling in his side-wallet. Impatient to enter I raise my palm to the door pad.

'No!' He grabs my wrist. 'It's offline. I have a key.'

'A what?'

He pulls a tool from his wallet, inserts it into a hole, turns it and then opens the door manually. 'After you.'

I'm not too sure about this. Going home with a stranger is fine, normally. Every door-entry and exit is recorded on our bar-codes and sent to the relevant data-base. If I enter this place, my recorder will have no idea where I am, where I've been.

The Dark Blue's eyes are gleaming naturally in the jaundiced moonlight. 'In you go. I dare you.'

The interior is reassuringly familiar. The standard layout for singles. I glance up into the corners of the room and feel at first comforted by the regulation number of recording devices. Until I realise that when I lift my hand there are no red lights blinking in response to the movement.

'Your vodcams are offline too?'

'Guess so. Fancy a drink?'

'Why isn't the offline alarm ringing?'

'I fixed that. I'm having a twist-and-dry. Join me?'

'It's illegal to tamper.'

'Oops. Go on, just a little one,'

I guess I should leave but he does have a nice smile and my throat is dry and I have to admit that I'm feeling strangely excited by being unwatched, unheard, unprotected.

'Okay. But let's get on with it. My data-input deadline's coming up in an hour or so.'

He puts his drink down and cups my chin in his hand. 'Enough of the sweet-talk, darling.'

His touch is odd. Tentative. I think the word is 'tender'. A tender touch.

I raise my palm. He looks in my eyes and lifts his palm in greeting.

And we connect.

And there's nothing. There's a black void of non-information that sends me reeling. Nothing. Just his hazel eyes and his warm skin against mine.

No past. No data. I don't know where he works, what he likes or who he's had.

'Impossible!'

'I fixed that, too.'

'How? What about your recorder? Data-gaps are always followed up.'

'Not always. People fall off the edge. Into a space. Anything can be arranged, if you know how.'

'Well that's it then.' I pull away. 'This is over.'

'It doesn't have to be.'

'Yes it does. I know nothing about you.'

He reaches out and takes me in his arms. 'Won't it be fun though? Finding out for yourself.'

Oh, it was more than fun. It was like making love to a virgin. Everything I did to him could have been for the first time. I'd whisper, 'Do you like this?' He'd murmur, 'What about this?' And no one was watching. No one was listening. It was like it had never happened.

It's time to leave now. I'm feeling strange. Like a White again. He leads me to the train-point and kisses me gently. 'Let's do this again.'
'We can't.'
'Why not?'
'There'll be consequences.'
'For who?'
'Me. My recorder will spot the gaps in transmission. I'll be reported.'
'No you won't.'
'Have you fixed that too?'
'Yes, Cary.'
I haven't told him my birthname. This information is only given to our recorders. Even in the most intimate moments shared between strangers the use of our secret names is forbidden.

I realise now that he knows everything about me. He knows my daily routines, my dark pleasures, The Light Blue and all the other shades before her.

My recorder smiles. 'I can take the real you offline for good, Cary. I'm good at fiction. If you don't tell, I won't.'

It takes less than a minute for me to decide. It might be tricky, dangerous and complicated and I know that, in time, someone will catch up with us but for the time being and for as long as I'm able…

I'm checking out.

About the author: Denise Hayes teaches at Newman University College, Birmingham, UK. She is inspired by facts, jokes and her favourite authors J.G. Ballard, Jorge Luis Borges and Philip K Dick. She has published poems in Hearing Voices and Mslexia and flash fiction in the Salt anthology Overheard: Stories to Read Aloud.

Infinite Maze by Leonie Ewing

*'The real universe could be lost amid an
infinite regress of nested fakes.'* -Paul Davies

On the threshold of the multi-entrance infinite maze Ariadne could not make up her mind which tunnel to chose. The more she peered into one hole after another, each darker than the last, the harder it got.

Choices, choices.

Finally she took the plunge, opting for the nearest entrance. Some unknown force held her above the surface of the passageway's fragile looking network which rippled around her, responding to her presence as she travelled along. Soft light kept pace with her, glowing pink as she advanced and dimming behind her. Ahead the tunnel branched.

Another choice to be made. Time to use my ball of string, then I think we'll turn

right. Just loop this through the network and make it fast. There. Quite secure.

Ariadne turned down the right fork unwinding the string as she went. Exploring

mazes was all part of a normal day's work. She fixed on the task ahead, no time for day dreaming. She was a creature of the present moment though occasionally she would experience vague, unsettling memory traces which did not tally with her current self-image. Perhaps it had something to do with the frequent teleportations she had undergone on her missions, her old self imperfectly copied, discrepancies accumulating, leaving shadows of previous incarnations.

There were other disturbing things too. Some days, as if she was listening to a

badly tuned radio, she would pick up faint conversations in her head. It was always between the same two people, Bob and Alice, and the only thing they ever discussed was feedback on the spin state of elementary particles. These particles were mysteriously entangled even though, as far as she could make out, Bob and Alice were at opposite ends of the universe.

Ariadne had always worked alone so she liked hearing Bob and Alice in her head.

It was company and there was something about the way they spoke to each other which suggested a connection beyond their work. She wondered what it would be like to have a partner.

Big mistake. The right fork ended in a cul-de-sac. No exit anywhere and in this case no turning back either. Panic gripped her. Nothing like this had ever happened before. She could make no sense of it. One step into the chamber and her legs had disappeared through the floor only to reappear through the ceiling. Equally confusing, her outstretched arms passed through the surface in front of her and reappeared through the surface behind her as if somehow she had been folded over and compressed like a suit in a parcel.

How to control my movements? I must get the hang of it or I'll be stuck here forever. Oh no! I don't believe it! The surface in front of me, it's transparent, that's... me! Endless copies of my back fading into the distance. The same on all sides. Now I'm too hot, burning up.

For once Ariadne's intelligent frictionless suit was at a loss as to what to do and switched itself off.

This space, it's shrinking, closing in fast. Think girl, think! Yes! The string. Shut my eyes. Concentrate. Rewind. I can do it...

She found herself back at the fork in the tunnel. Her suit began to apologise for being useless but Ariadne ignored it. She let out the string again then took a left turn. No sooner had she settled down to a steady pace than she felt a tug behind her. She turned round to see two fluffy kittens, lit up by a show of changing colours, rolling around together and tangled up in the string. She tugged sharply until it was taut and the pair ran off hissing.

Well, looks like Schrödinger's cat must have survived after all. Now, if I keep taking only left forks from now on maybe I'll arrive back at the start. This is more like it. At last I'm back in my sort of territory.

The tunnel narrowed gradually and began to curl up. Ariadne tucked and dived, flipped, twisted and turned, bent and stretched her supple body so it flowed smoothly through the compactified spaces. This was Ariadne's sensuous reward for her work. As she performed, the network constantly adjusted to her passage and the string undulating in her wake gave off tiny electric sparks.

In the Great Hall, Members of the Committee for the Mathematics of Hyperspace were scanning a bank of screens. A deep frown creased the Chairman's brow. He was exceedingly angry. He turned to the Members.

'Well, at least Ariadne managed to extricate herself but as for you lot, I demand an explanation! How in the cosmos could a Misner space have got into the hyper-dimensional space programme? A miracle she escaped before the entire space collapsed in on her. A nanosecond more and she would have fried. One of our most experienced navigators. We simply can't afford to lose her. And as for those kittens, how do you account for that?'

No-one answered though the Senior Fellow, well known for her love of felines, did look away. The rest of them tracked the stream of electrons escaping from the synthetic polymer string that marked Ariadne's passage through the curled up dimensions of hyperspace.

As they watched, Ariadne executed a particularly graceful triple somersault with a double twist. The Chairman, who had been scrolling down a table of prime knots on his split screen, shouted at his computer to freeze the moving trace. Anger gone, he beamed at his colleagues.

'At last, the first new knot of the century! Perfectly beautiful. What's more, the first ever knot with *fourteen* crossings. It will need to be checked of course, but I think this calls for a celebration.'

The Committee, except for the Junior Fellow who continued to study Ariadne's progress through the maze, crowded round the Chairman's screen to admire the new object and talk about the need to publish the finding quickly before the opposition caught up.

On the Junior Fellow's screen something strange was happening. The flowing ribbon of light marking Ariadne's passage had come to a standstill and all that could be seen was one bright spot slowly increasing in size. What was Ariadne doing? Instantly the young man called up the tunnel map and scrolled the overlay until the coordinates matched.

Ariadne was nowhere near the maze entrance, which was where he expected to find her, but in a remote region he did not recognise. There was, however, something horribly familiar about the behaviour of the light on the screen. Without hesitating he leaned forward and flipped the main switch. All the screens went blank. There was a roar of protest from the other Members. He looked at them helplessly.

'I had to. She'd found a wormhole. And don't ask me how it got there.'

Upstairs in his loft-conversion bedroom a teen-aged boy was sitting at his PC with half an eye on the screen. He was listening to surround-sound music through a wireless connection to miniature receivers in his ears and simultaneously texting on his phone. Occasionally he would break off to tap the computer screen and tweak the programme he was developing. He had not heard his mother calling him to supper but now he did hear the loud bang on his door so he saved, then closed the file he was working on. Instantly the light went out on the Committee for the Mathematics of Hyperspace.

Ariadne exited the wormhole at the Casimir Gates. She had never been out of doors in any of her previous existences. She stood blinking in strong sunlight still clutching her ball of string like a child with its comforter. She raised her hand to shield her eyes from the glare and scanned the scene. At the edge of a line of dark, needle-sharp trees something moved. A tall figure strode towards her stirring up ochre dust as it advanced, a man strangely dressed in a kind of kilted tunic. As he drew closer Ariadne could see he was smiling in a friendly way even though he carried a sword. Her intelligent suit turned a pretty pink then morphed into a loose shift with a flouncy skirt.

'Ah, you must be Ariadne,' said the man.' My name is Theseus. I'm here on the Minotaur Project. It seems we're to be partners.'

With a shy smile Ariadne stepped forward and shook Theseus by the hand.

About the author: Leonie Ewing is a retired biologist and farmer who enjoys reading popular physics and SF. She also writes poetry and has had her work published in a number of literary magazines including Southlight and Markings.

The Trouble With Dragons by Danuta Reah

The trouble with dragons is they are dangerous.

I knew that, even before the dragons came to the wild place. The wild place is just down the road from our estate. It's between some old shops and a car park. There's a fence round it, but it's old and saggy. Us kids play there a lot, even though there's still a sign that says Keep out.

The wild place is dangerous because someone could have an accident.

Dragons are a different matter. Dragons are dangerous because they mean to be.

They came to the wild place one Sunday night, or at least they were there on Monday morning when I walked past it to school. Someone had built a dragon pen with bright new signs: Danger. Deep Excavation, and Danger. Work in Progress. I peered through the cage bars and I saw them.

Dragons aren't like the books tell you. They are all different colours and different shapes and sizes. These dragons were yellow. There was a long, lean one with huge jaws like steel. It was eating the ground when I first saw it. It reared its head up high, calling out in its dragon voice: Rrraargh! Rrraargh! There was a small fat one as well, and it rumbled round the ground pushing the piles of earth the big dragon had left. This dragon didn't seem so fierce and it had a gentle voice that went something like Bbbrrrm. I kind of liked it.

I couldn't wait to tell my friend, Richard. Richard lives next door. His mum died a few months ago, and his uncle came to live with him. I don't like Richard's uncle. He comes to our house a lot and sits on the sofa with mum. They drink wine together and laugh, but every time I look at him, he's watching me so I mostly stay outside when he's there.

Mum didn't want me around when Mr Holly was there anyway so Richard and I used to go and play in the wild place. Now it didn't look as if there was anywhere we could go.

The trouble with dragons is when they move in, everyone else has to keep away.

Richard wasn't in school that day. 'Where's Richard Holly? Is he away *again*?' the teacher said, and her voice went all sarcastic when she said 'again.' After his mum died, the teacher used to say, Well, it's understandable, but now they seemed to think Richard should be OK about his mum, especially now his uncle was here.

David Holly is a lovely man. It's good when family stick together, I heard our teacher say once, and I wondered if it was only me who could see that no one would want Mr Holly sticking to them. A few weeks ago, Richard played football for the first time since his mother died. He scored a goal, skidding over the tarmac of the playground and tearing his shirt. Everyone cheered. The next day, he was ill again and he didn't come to school for three days.

After that, he said he didn't want to play football anymore.

I made a mistake then. Because Richard wasn't there, I told Lily who I sometimes play with about the dragons. 'Dragons? There's no such thing,' she said. Then she told some of the others, so everyone was going Dragons! Look who believes in dragons. Even the teacher laughed a bit and said, 'You're a bit too old to believe in fairies,' which wasn't what I'd said at all. I could see it was going to be dragons and fairies all week until they'd got something else to talk about. I didn't take Lily back past the wild place and I didn't show her them.

The trouble with dragons is if people don't believe in them then they can't see them.

On the way home, I stopped by the dragon's pen. There was another dragon now. The long lean one with the steel jaws was still there. It had glittering eyes, and I didn't think it would be friendly. I thought the small fat one might be, but it was dozing in the sun. The new dragon was big with a huge head and an open mouth. Its head went round and round. I didn't like the look of that one. It looked dangerous to me.

I climbed up on the fence to try and see a bit more, but one of the dragon keepers saw me and shouted. I jumped down and ran home. Mum was standing in the doorway talking to one of the neighbours. '...Noise and dust all summer, I suppose.' She saw me. 'What have you been up to?'

'What's for tea?' I said. I was hungry, and there was no point in telling her about the dragons.

'Oh, go and look,' she said.

I could hear her talking as I went inside. '...Supermarket, they say. And a pub. That place been an eyesore since they pulled the old petrol station down...' I hoped the dragons weren't going to turn the whole of the wild place into a supermarket.

There wasn't much for tea. The bread was dry. I put some spread on it and ate that, and some biscuits. I was still hungry, but there wasn't anything else.

I wanted to go and see Richard Holly, but I didn't want to see his uncle. I went out onto the street and kicked a stone up and down, and after a while, he came out.

'Hello, Richard,' one of the neighbours called. 'How are you? How's your uncle?'

Richard muttered something and put his hands in his pockets. I said, 'Want to come to the wild place?'

He shook his head. 'I'm not allowed. I'm... poorly.'

He was moving a bit slowly, as if something was hurting him.

'Was that why you weren't at school?'

He nodded. He looked miserable. His face looked thin and white, not round and pink like it was when his mum was alive.

'Are you alright?' I asked

'Course.' He shrugged.

'Listen,' I said. 'I knew something that would cheer him up. I was a bit afraid he would be like Lily and the others, but I told him anyway. 'There's dragons. In the wild place.'

'You're kidding me. Not *really*.'

I nodded my head. Really dragons.

'Dragons? Cool.' He grinned, then his face went still. I looked behind me, and there was Mr Holly just standing watching us with that look on his face. He smelt of the after shave he wore when he came to see Mum. 'Hey, curly top.' He always calls me 'curly top' which I hate. It's like he can't be bothered to remember my name. 'I've got something to show you. Got this great new game on my Playstation. Want to come and see it?'

Richard looked at me and shook his head.

'No,' I said.

'No, what?' said Mr Holly.

'No I don't want to come and see your new game.'

'Not good enough for you, curly top? Is that it.'

Richard looked scared, so I said, 'I've got to ask my mum. I can't come and see it now.'

Then he smiled, and there was something about his smile that made me feel cold. 'OK. Later.' He got hold of Richard's shoulder. 'In,' he said.

Richard's face was white and funny as Mr Holly pushed him towards their front door.

I watched as the door closed behind them. I didn't want to think about what Mr Holly's smile meant. Instead, I went back to the wild place and watched the dragons. They were sitting quietly in a friendly group, and though I knew they were dangerous, I kind of wished I was sitting there with them. If I had dragon friends, Mr Holly wouldn't look at me in that funny way. And he wouldn't hurt Richard.

It was almost dark. Suddenly, the dragons opened their eyes, sending a glare of light across the wild place. I looked for the little fat one, but all I could see was their eyes in the darkness and all I could hear was a low growl. I didn't know if they were being friendly, or if they were angry. Maybe they didn't like me there watching them. 'I'm sorry if I disturbed you,' I said. I decided I'd better go.

The trouble with dragons is you can never tell what they are thinking.

When I got home, Mum was putting on her make-up. 'Where have you been? Do you know what time it is? I'm going out with the girls. I want you in bed before I go. Mr Holly said he'd pop in and make sure you're OK.'

'You never...' I began to say. I wanted to say that Mum never bothered with anyone to look after me before, but she gave me a look and I stopped. 'I don't want Mr Holly to come in. I'll be fine.'

'Well, he offered, so you'll just have to put up with it.'

'I don't like Mr Holly.'

Mum was smiling in the mirror, but it was just so she could put lipstick on her mouth. When she spoke, her voice was cross. 'Don't be so stupid.'

'But Mum, I *don't* like him. He's horrible to Richard, He...' I couldn't think of a way to say what I wanted to tell her. Richard had made me promise not to tell. 'He's funny with me. He looks at me like...'

Smack! Her hand moved so quickly I couldn't get out of the way. I was scared of the expression on her face. I realised she knew what I was going to say, and she didn't want to hear it. 'You're always causing trouble, you,' she said.

My ear stung from the slap. Mum's face was up close to mine. The skin was creased and dry and the make-up was flaking off. She shook me. 'Don't you tell such wicked lies!' she hissed. 'Don't let me hear stories like that from you again! You little...' She stopped. 'I haven't got time for this. I'm late.' The front door slammed behind her.

I wiped my eyes with my hands a couple of times as I stood there. Mum knew, but she was pretending not to know, even to herself. She liked Mr Holly. She liked the times they spent together drinking wine. She liked the way he took her out sometimes in his car. She thought Mr Holly was doing it because he liked her, but I knew it was something else. I sat there for a long time, trying to think what to do.

Then I heard a sound at the door. It was the key, rattling a bit as someone tried to fit it into the lock. I remembered what Mum said. Mr Holly was going to come over and see if I was alright. He was at the door now.

I stood there for a second, frozen, then I ran to the back door and out into the night. I didn't know where to go. I didn't know where Mum had gone and she didn't want to listen anyway.

Richard. Richard knew. Richard would believe me. Richard would help.

I could hear Mr Holly calling. 'Hey, curly top? Where've you got to?'

I was in his yard now. It was pitch dark. I crept to the house and looked up at the windows. The small one next to the bathroom, that was Richard's. I scooped up some pebbles from the ground and threw them. They landed with a rattle and I threw some more.

Richard's face appeared at the window. I beckoned, mouthing 'Come down! Come down.'

He just looked at me for a moment, then he nodded. I saw him turn away, and a few seconds later, I heard the front door of his house open and I crept down the path towards the gate.

'There you are, curly top!' I spun round. Mr Holly was standing behind me. He was smiling. 'Oh now this won't do. Outside in the night? I'll have to deal with you.'

He staggered and almost fell over. Richard was there. He'd come running up the path and crashed as hard as he could into Mr Holly.

I grabbed his hand. 'Come on!' And we both ran.

I had no idea where we were running to. I don't think Richard did either. We were on the street, running as fast as we could, and I could hear Mr Holly's feet, slap, slap, slap on the pavement behind us, getting closer and closer.

'I can't...' Richard's face was pale and he was clutching his stomach. Before I could do anything, I felt My Holly's hand grab me. 'Oh, I'm going to have to deal with both of you.' His face looked pleased, but it looked awful as well. I pulled back to get away, and I felt the mesh of the dragons' pen press into my back. I saw his belt was undone, and I remembered the way Richard couldn't run.

I did the only thing I could. I looked into the darkness where the dragons were. 'Please?' I whispered.

And the lights glared out as the dragons opened their eyes. The roaring started and this time I knew they were angry, very angry. I didn't know who they were angry with. Maybe it was me, but I didn't care.

Mr Holly stood there in the light from their eyes. He looked – not scared, but puzzled. 'What the fu...' he began.

Then the great steel jaws of the tall dragon reached over the top of the pen. They gripped Mr Holly round his waist. He shouted out as the dragon lifted him up high. I saw the great neck swing round, and the dragon's jaws opened, dropping Mr Holly into the hole the dragons had dug.

Then the dragon the scared me most came forward. Its turning head tipped as it peered into the hole, and it breathed out.

Not all dragons breathe fire. The turning head dragon breathed stuff like grey mud that came streaming out of its mouth, down and down and down into the hole where Mr Holly lay.

Then the dragon lifted its turning head up to the sky, and everything was quiet.

There was just the wild place, and the dragons, and the silence.

Then the dragons came out of their pen. You can't keep dragons caged if they don't want to be. 'Come on,' I said to Richard. We climbed up onto the small, fat dragon. I put my arms round its neck, then we sat on its back in the leather saddle, and the dragons went away. When they went, Richard Holly and I went with them.

The trouble with dragons is sometimes they're real.

About the author: Danuta Reah is one of our professional contributors who also writes as Carla Banks and has published many novels and several short stories. In 2005 she won the Crime Writers' Association Short Story Dagger for her story No Flies on Frank. Her latest book, Not Safe, a novella, explores the dangers facing asylum seekers in a South Yorkshire city.

Visit her website at; www.danutareah.com

FUSION

Baby Babble by John Hoggard

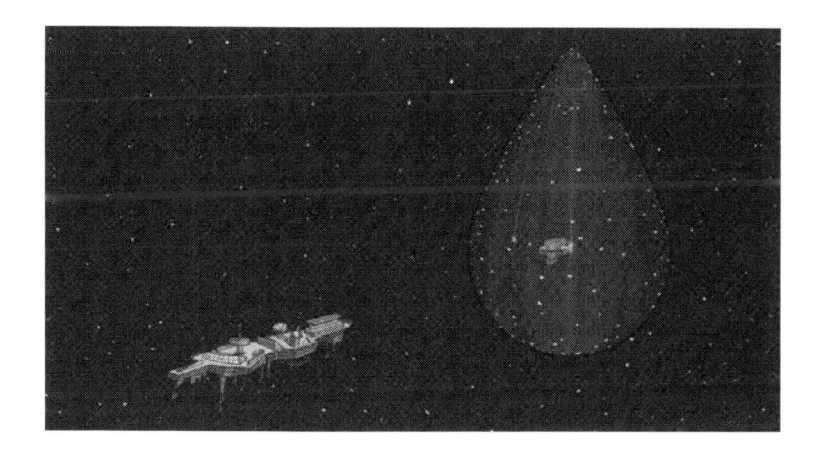

The ship hung above the Earth that had created it like a giant, old style compass needle, pointing towards the stars and potential salvation. It was now so large that it was visible even during the day to the naked eye. People had stared into the night sky for the last fifteen years of construction and knew its sequence of running lights as well as the constellations.

The engines of *Last Hope* had been charging for two years. The vast solar collector had dimmed the sun, its shadow briefly turning daylight to twilight as each day it raced across the world below. Soon, the most complicated computers humankind had ever constructed would pour that energy into a new and untested engine that would rip a hole in the fabric of space and throw the ship into the unknown.

The engine reached fully charged just three days before the 'must jump' deadline and that's terribly close for a project that had been the sole focus for the Earth's population for two generations and had the blood of thousands of lives weaved into the fabric of its existence. The ship's Commander issued the order to begin the launch sequence and two years worth of collected solar energy poured into a spot no bigger than a grain of sand and a new, tiny sun burst into life in the heart of the vessel. The Commander allowed himself the briefest of smiles. This ship, this mission really was his. The years of politics and fighting with the military to hold on to this position were behind him. He was a master of communication but he had struggled to make them listen, let alone understand.

The ship pushed off and headed for interplanetary space, past the moon and the vast engineering works that had fabricated it, beyond the asteroid belt picked clean of minerals and isotopes and out to Jupiter. It was hoped that the Gas Giant might shield planet Earth from the effects of the experimental Fold Engine when it was finally engaged. If time had allowed, the scientists knew how to improve the engine, but there was no more time.

Scientists were right to be concerned. The beautiful atmospheric banding and magnificent Red Spot are torn apart as the shock wave from the Fold Engine's discharge slam into the Gas Giant. *Last Hope* has ripped a hole in the fabric of space and left Jupiter, an innocent victim of that assault, scarred, perhaps for eternity.

Last Hope is unaware of the damage it has done, it may not know for a very long time, as the quantum-entanglement communication system, is non-functional. If this meeting goes badly, it will never know.

Trillions of mathematical computations confirm that *Last Hope* has arrived at the pre-chosen coordinates. Billions more, confirm the ship is intact, the fusion reactors are still on line and recharging the depleted but still functional Fold Engine. It will still take two hours of probing with the finest, most sensitive sensors ever constructed to detect the other vessel. Two hours for the Commander to think about why he is here, to wonder why his extraordinary gift was his and his alone, to wonder if he is really up to the task. The other ship is the reason *Last Hope* is here, the reason she exists at all.

The moment the Earth ship's sensors settle on their target the other ship moves to intercept. They have clearly been watching and waiting. Perhaps the first stage of the test has been passed. The crew and Commander wait nervously. At a range of ten million kilometres every weapon system of the Earth ship comes on line and powers up. It is a lethal cocktail of nuclear tipped missiles, lasers and neutron cannons, but it will do the Earth ship no good at all. The Commander of *Last Hope* already knows that his weapons are useless against the other vessel, an entire fleet of ships discovered that almost sixty years ago, and sixty years has been no time at all to improve the lethality of human weapons to the level required to alter that, despite the bravado and bluster of the military back home. The Commander also knows that his own ship; the toughest ever constructed could be vaporised in an instant. Scientists have had sixty years to study what the other ship did to Pluto as it left the Sol system, sixty years to stare agog at the calculated power figures and to be afraid.

He had fought the military all the way but the weapons had remained part of the design and now he knew why. The military chiefs said that he should lie, say that the weapons were purely for defensive purposes should the *Last Hope* encounter anything else while awaiting the rendezvous. But the Commander explained as best he could to closed minds that could not understand or comprehend what he was trying to tell them. He told them he could not lie, that the chosen form of communication would not allow it. He told them words, not weapons, would save Humankind, all they had to do was build a ship to get him there and he could prove it.

They had built the ship but it appears that they did not believe him, the weapons are on automatic, he has no control of them at all. He is grateful that the range of his communication system is much greater than the range of the weapons. He will at least have a short time to try and establish contact.

As the other ship reaches the edge of communication range he has time now, to study it as the screen before him powers up and the computers calculate the algorithms necessary to keep the signal strong and undistorted. There would be no fanciful *universal translators* here, just words, carefully chosen, but just words nonetheless, produced by his own vocal cords and nothing else.

The two ships are very different. *Last Hope* is long and thin, covered in antenna and bulbous protrusions and lights. She looks like a cross between a giant aircraft carrier and an oil rig. The alien ship is enormous, ten times the volume of the Earth ship. It is smooth as glass, tear drop shaped, beautiful. They have clearly been doing this for a long time.

The communications officer confirms that they are on transmit for both audio and video streams. Soon the other ship will move into weapons range and the Commander is fearful that the *Last Hope* will pre-empt him and open fire. He has waited for this moment, quite literally, his entire life. He was born into a house where his father, a world renowned linguistic specialist, battled with the transmissions left behind by the alien vessel. He had listened to them constantly. They were as familiar to him as his mother's own soothing tones. It was his father who noticed that somehow he understood the messages. Later, when he was older and had the vocabulary, he tried to explain. It turned out this understanding was his and his alone, it was unteachable, despite his best efforts with hundreds of carefully chosen military officers and to the absolute fury of the military who accused him of lying and manipulation to retain control of the project and eventually the ship.

The Commander takes a slow calming breath, pushes aside every thought except the job in hand. He focuses on the inner voice and lets it bubble up.

'Da da burr da bo ga ba ba cla bu ba,' he gurgles in a happy sing-song voice, rocking backwards and forwards his arms flailing around in front of him. The rest of the ship's crew carry on their jobs flawlessly. They had been warned what to expect but this is the first time they will have seen the Commander actively trying to communicate.

For a terrifying moment there is no reply, no response of any kind, but then, at the point a cold chill of panic begins to set in, the screen brightens and he is presented with something that does not really seem to have a head or arms, or anything vaguely comparative to human appendages and there is a voice that is deep and rasping and yet also reciprocates that strange sing-songy tone and the *tendrils* flail in a similar manner to the commander's own arms.

He understands. With absolute clarity and certainty he understands.

They understand too.

He explains about the weapons.

They understand. They are not concerned. The alien ship halts outside weapons range of *Last Hope*. They have time to talk.

The commander is delighted. Talk, baby babble, the true universal language, not weapons or technology will save the human race this day.

About the author: John Hoggard has been writing since at least the age of six, when a local newspaper printed one of his science-fiction stories. Buoyed by this early success he has been writing science-fiction ever since. His wife and two children tolerate his periods of absence, while he stares, frustrated, at a blank screen.

Follow John on Twitter: @DaddyHoggy

Metal by Drew Wagar

The planet recedes rapidly in the viewport as I gaze upon it. It is a world of serene beauty, harking back to how Earth must have been before humanity spread across its face like an unchecked infection.

We came in response to a distress call from an early survey ship. Its crew had been tasked with searching out other worlds we could plunder, a mission we continue to this day; a desperate scramble to slake our thirst for metal. Lost before I was born, that ship was little more than a minor footnote until a chance pass by a probe picked up its faint beacon. The planet had long since been deleted from our portfolio. It was lacking in metals, suitable only for a simple agrarian culture, irrelevant to the high industry that drove our civilization.

On entering orbit we found that the survey ship had landed, a contravention of laws governing exploration at the time, as it was suspected that the planet supported higher forms of life, perhaps even intelligence.

We could get nothing from the automated systems aboard. Our cameras gave us a low-res image of the ship's broken carcass on a hillside. A plume of pale white material fanned out from the wreck, fading into the greenery after a few miles. Most of us thought it was some sort of windblown sand that had accumulated in the lee of the wreck. Our chief scientist proposed a form of coral attracted to the metals of the old survey ship.

Descent was a leisurely process. We cautiously dropped our scout ship into the atmosphere, stopping at various points to check and confirm our position and estimates. Not for us the tense fiery plunge though the atmosphere that original survey crew would have endured.

We had a strict agenda; other worlds beckoned, and the Consortium paid us to find resources to support humanity's endless expansion, not to solve ancient mysteries. We had terse instructions to retrieve the survey ship's memory core and then proceed with our work.

We landed someway clear of the wreck and spent a moment checking atmospheric pressure, temperature and composition. Everything was routine. It wasn't a parallel Earth by any stretch of the imagination, but short exposure wouldn't cause any lasting effects to our crew.

The atmosphere felt thin and dry. Overhead a pale azure sky stretched from horizon to horizon, a strange but oddly comforting sight, like those disputed images of Earth from the early-tech era.

Beneath our booted feet a velvet carpet of moss-like vegetation covered the hillside. Dark green plants grew absurdly tall and spindly in the low gravity. We could hear no birds or insect life. Apprehension gave way to bemusement as we acclimatised to an almost complete lack of noise, save the faint rustle as the breeze gently swayed the fragile vegetation.

The wreck's squat metallic form, a series of incongruous sharp edges and straight panels, was a jarring contrast to the soft curves of the landscape it had impaled. Immediately we could see that it had crashed, the forward nose cone buckled and bent upwards, the ship twisted halfway down its length, spilling the contents of its hold away from our vantage point. The hull was tarnished and scored. The plume of white material was on the far side of the hill, hidden by the ship's dark bulk.

We'd read stories of those days, of course. A primitive ship manned by a highly trained crew chosen for toughness, endurance and versatility. Rations were mean and living conditions intolerable to our modern sensibilities.

We continued up the hill, still conscious of the silence. It was as if we were intruders in a carefully manicured garden. Any moment the grounds-keeper might appear, dealing out severe punishment for trespassers. I noticed we all stepped lightly, as if trying not to harm the spongy moss beneath our feet, if so, it was an act of respect agreed by an unspoken pact.

On reaching the stricken vessel we each laid a hand on its stained and tarnished flanks. I don't know about the others, but I felt compelled to connect with what must have been a terrifying tragedy all those years ago. The ships' systems were wrecked beyond hope of economic repair. Only the faint pulsing of the beacon remained. We traced our way round the perimeter of the ship.

The contents of the hold, its cargo of precious metals, lay strewn across the ground. We were elated at this. Already plans for its retrieval began forming in my mind. Then we raised our eyes.

The sight that greeted us on the far side will haunt my dreams until I'm recycled, too worn to be replaced, too uneconomic to sustain. I struggle to convey the utter horror with which we contemplated the vista before us.

Stretching from the shattered hull of the survey ship, down the far side of the hill and carrying on to where the faint mist determined the limits of vision, the white 'material' lay. There were gasps, some cried out in alarm, others involuntarily stepped back losing their balance.

Bones. Endless bones, bleached white by the system's fierce little star. Bones as far as the eye could see.

Delicate creatures they must have been. They were as tall as we humans and of similar construction, yet far less substantial in their build. We saw lone adults and family groups. That they were intelligent was obvious, this was no accidental mass grave by some strange affliction. Despite some disturbance from the wind over the centuries, it was clear the remains were all aligned, with legs set straight and arms pointing towards the wreck. Their bodies lay on their backs, empty eye sockets staring into the heavens. An arc of bodies all paying some ghastly ancient homage to our ancestors' utilitarian wreck.

They were primitive people, with basic stone tools and meagre resources. What they must have made of the crashing impact of our survey vessel into their world I don't know, but they came to revere and worship it as some form of deity. They must have observed the scattered contents of the hold and determined that their new god deemed these metals of high worth; we found lumps of ore and fragments of metal clasped in the hands of many of the people. Later we found evidence of simple mining; they had gone to great lengths to offer what they had.

I found one skeleton, a female as it turned out, closest to the wreckage. She was set slightly apart, and not arranged like the others, but untidily strewn on her side, with a single arm outstretched in a silent plea, her back arched, a smattering of coloured stones clasped in her hand. A thin sliver of sharpened rock lay alongside her; a primitive knife. Was she slave or sacrifice? The priestess of their culture? A Queen perhaps?

I hold those worthless stones in my hand now, whilst my colleagues talk and laugh, and our vessel returns to the mission assigned to it. Those people tried to appease this new god with offerings, at unconscionable cost to themselves.

Perhaps they thought that some great revelation awaited them once their offering was deemed sufficient. Yet, when there was no more metal left for them to find they gave whatever they had; those pitiful pointless gifts of ore, rock and stone. Finally, they gave themselves.

Their god never answered, utterly indifferent to their plight.

About the author: Drew Wagar has been an avid sci-fi and fantasy fan since childhood. He has published a four-part space-opera, a contemporary novel and is currently working on a new fantasy series. He is also the author of Elite: Reclamation and is joining FBP with his latest series, the Shadeward Saga.

Dust to Dust by Polly Robinson

Tansy sat watching the dusty, scabby, eccentric guy tinkering with a dirty old computer.

He kept muttering, 'All that's left.'

Tansy, through the mists of a headache, thought he must be mad. How could he know what was left? He was old. Very, very old. She focused her fading eyes on him; concentrating until the image solidified. He looked at least 200, his puckered, peeling skin like burnt paper at the edges, his smell reminding her unpleasantly of spent matches. Her lungs tingled and her mouth was parched; every breath scorched her throat; her head hurt.

'Garam,' she croaked, oblivious that she had been repeating the name periodically for more than 48 hours. Nothing.

The ventowave said Europe and America had declared peace, its pocket-sized chassis pitted and scored by acidic dust that blew across the River Thames from time to time as if some great god were sighing over remnants. Nothing left of the Eastern Bloc. All desert, they said, little water. The world now half the size ... She'd fought for the ventowave, clawing beneath rubble a foot deep, breaking fingernails, grazing knuckles, she'd even poked someone in the eye to get at the grey plastic radio first – they'd disappeared into thin air, there one minute gone the next.

'Garam,' she croaked again.

'Stop bawling, girl,' said the eccentric, 'can't you see I'm busy? Why don't you help or go and look for your Garam?'

She glared at him, seeing that the tool he used on the computer wreck was a metal nail file.

'Have you no proper tools?' she asked, feeling her lips crack and bleed with the effort.

'I have this,' he said holding the file up, 'And this,' he gestured toward the computer.

'What's happening?' Tansy asked. 'D'you think it's stopped or will it get worse, the dust and ..?'

'It's stopped for now,' he said, more kindly than she expected, 'I just need to make one small connection and then we can find out what's ha ...' he was interrupted by the crackle of the ventowave.

'Turn it up, girl,' he said, taking a step towards her. She shrank back. 'Turn it up so I can hear it.'

The disembodied voice proclaimed, 'This is the World Service, 11 August 2389. Reports are coming in ... shsssshsssh ..,' crackling, nothing.

'We'll have to wait for the next one,' she whispered, 'I'm Tansy. Who are you?'

'Eric. Eric Hawsley. Pleased to meet you Tansy,' he held out a burned, crazed hand. She looked at it for a moment before taking it in her own.

'Have you seen Garam?' she asked.

'What's he like?' Eric returned to his computer. She wanted to say: tall and dark, but that would be as good as no description and who was to say what he'd look like now? She was different; she looked at her hands, crazed, like a crackle glaze, just like a raku crackle glaze, just like Eric's.

'Have you spoken to any of the Reptilators?' Eric asked.

'You're the first being I've spoken to since ...'

'You know they're claiming power?' he interrupted.

'The Reptilators?'

'They're saying ...' he cursed as the metal file snapped, the sharp end flying up and gouging his cheek. 'Damn,' he brushed slimy pink blood from his face. 'They're saying they planned the whole thing, that they made peace with America.

If we support them we live, if we don't ..,' he continued to fidget with valves and co-axial cable.

'But it's not them on the airwaves,' protested Tansy, 'people in power always take control of the airwaves first.'

'How many ventowaves do you think there are, Tansy?' asked Eric, his cynical grin emphasising the grotesque mask of a face. 'The only information comes from others before they ..,' he didn't finish the sentence as the computer buzzed into life. 'Ah-ha!' scales of skin fell from his face. He tapped commands on the keyboard. The wound on his face continued to drip pink viscous pus-like fluid. Tansy couldn't help herself, she moved further away, pain shooting through her legs as she rose.

'Are you going for food?' Eric asked, intent on the screen.

'I will. There's plenty about.'

'Look out for Reptilators,' he warned, 'they move so quietly they'll be on you before you know, and those fire-guns are lethal, burn you to a crisp before you even hear them.'

She left the ventowave with him – more as a guarantee she'd be back than anything – turned and slowly picked her way through the rubble away from Trafalgar Square. It was a gentle irony, she grimaced, that Napoleon, having usurped Nelson for the past two centuries peering over the French colony of London, should now be lying, tricorne smashed, as much a broken man as he was after Waterloo.

The boulevard seemed deserted. Whirling, searing dust-ridden air clogged her failing vision. Tansy could sense rather than see movements in the shadows. Makeshift tents were formed from chequered blankets thrown over upturned bins and dissected lampposts. There were no dead. Where were the dead? A hint of suspicion nudged at her. She pushed it to the back of her mind. The dust was cloying, making each breath painful, the ash biting and cold, nipping, pinching at her face and arms. She coughed. It got everywhere, eyes, ears, skin, mouth, throat, lungs. She shuffled past the colonial buildings and the windows peered back at her blindly, no movement within.

Inside a store a scraping alerted her to another presence. Fear stopped her. One of the Reptilators? She flattened against a half-raided container.

'Come out of there! Whoever you are!' growled a ratchety voice. She didn't move. 'Come out or get incinerated.'

She couldn't see, tried to focus, made out the nozzle of a fire-gun edging toward her. Moving excruciatingly slowly, arms painfully raised, she eased around the corner to confront the holder of the fire-gun.

'Garam!' A finger of steel strapped itself around her head and squeezed. She was almost horrified to see him alive. With her nerves at screaming point she sobbed 'Oh, Garam, you're alive.'

'Tansy!' He looked as bad as she'd feared, even so she moved slowly into his outstretched arms and covered his flaking face with a multitude of kisses, ignoring the stench off his flesh and the weakness invading her legs.

'What are you doing with a fire-gun?' she asked, 'Where have you been? Where were you when it happened?'

'Hey, hey, one at a time,' he smiled and, as with Eric, the movement caused great wadges of skin to break free. 'Come on. Let's get out of here before …'

'I've got to take food to Eric,' Tansy explained about Eric and the computer he'd got working. Garam watched her collect what she needed, saw the agony in her face as she struggled to carry the bag, and took it from her. They set off back to Eric. Garam slowed his pace so that she could keep up with him.

'Where are the bodies?' she asked. He didn't reply, so she asked him again.

'There are none,' he finally said. They were almost back at Trafalgar Square. Tansy heard the computer. She placed a delicate, peeling hand on Garam's arm, stopping him in his tracks.

'Where are they?' she said and the suspicion she'd had earlier took shape. 'Are they the dust? The ash and dust?' Tears caught in her face.

'They are, Tansy,' Garam said gently, 'They're blowing over the Thames.' She turned away sickened; the dull sulphurous dust, all that was left, dust to dust. Another gust of searing wind brought with it a hail of acidic burning particles. Tansy held her head as more pain gripped her. Garam, his arm around her heaving shoulders, guided her to where Eric was staring fixedly at the screen.

'There are Eurobod's left in hiding,' said Eric without preamble, 'they have the airwaves. They're saved but stuck miles away in the country. They've no hope of running the continent from there. There aren't enough ventowaves working to let people know they're alive and the Reptilators have seized power with help from ...' Eric looked upwards.

'If some ministers are left, someone to oppose them,' Garam said hopefully.

'Too late my boy,' said Eric shaking his head, hair and scales floating from him like petals from a cherry tree. 'Too late. The Reptilators have got to the city first. They have control because they've taken it. They're here.' He sat down heavily no longer staring at the screen. Drawn to the screen, Garam and Tansy could make the word 'DELETE' stamped across it in huge green capital letters. Garam stiffened, Tansy fluttered down beside Eric, weeping silently.

'All's lost,' her frail voice tremored fading to an echo, 'ost ... ost ... ost ...' as she dustily drifted across the River Thames.

About the author: Polly Robinson is a member of Worcester Writers' Circle, Worcestershire Literary Festival, Parole Parlate and 42. Her writing has been published in anthologies such as the Survivor's Guide to Bedlam; Reflections on a Blue Planet: Earth – Water – Sky and Reflections on a Blue Planet: Nature's Palette (Wrixton & Hirst, 2012), Ripples: Friends in Verse (Summers, 2012), and

Eerie Digest (www.eeriedigest.com April, May, 2012). This is the first of two of Polly's stories in this anthology.

Read more about Polly on her blog at journalread.wordpress.com

The Flight of the Magician by Jonny Rowland

I saw him one night at a service station. I was stopping off to give my eyes a rest before I made the last leg of my trip home. My feet too – the old pair of black converses I wore had rubbed my ankles, even though I'd just been working car pedals. I'd only thought to spend a few minutes looking at magazines, but the moment the smell of chip fat stabbed my nose I had to eat. I picked up a plate of the toughest chips, bacon and beans I have ever seen. At that time of night, there were only two other customers, a thin Indian bloke with a plate of equally fat-laced chips and the one guy I didn't think would bother me. That was the man I'd later know as Barry.

He was about average height and wide around the shoulders. He had a head like a broad bean: a prominent brow with thick black eyebrows and a round chin you could use to smash nuts. He was the last person I would expect to be a talker. That was until he asked, matter-of-fact like, 'How old?'

'Twenty five.'

'Isn't that a bit much?' He gave me a bit of a smile.

'What do you mean?'

'They're probably changed after a day under the heater. I know the chips are old, but I don't think they're that old.'

'Oh. Thought you meant me.'

'Though judging by the taste, I'd say that your answer's probably closer to the truth than the truth is. Know what I mean?'

I nodded and got on with my meal, thinking he was done.

'So,' he continued, 'Where are you headed, Mr Twenty Five?'

'Home. It's been a long day's travel for me.'

'For you, maybe. There are truckers here that have washing machines to deliver. The kind that have to be in Cardiff by nine in the morning.'

'Sorry,' I said.

'Don't be. You're a day person, I'm a night person. I sleep when the sun shines. That's all the difference. In the end, we're all just travellers, trying to get somewhere.'

The Indian called over, 'I'd run now. Barry wants to tell the Magician story, and he won't let you leave once he's started it.'

Barry seemed to be waiting for the question, so I asked it. 'What magician story?'

'The Magician was a strange bloke,' said Barry, 'Only saw him a few times, but he was serious business.'

'And Barry likes any reason to shoehorn him into a conversation,' added the Indian.

'He was an enigma, Rav.'

'So, who was this Magician?' I asked the Indian guy.

'A free runner,' he said, in the same tone that you might say 'parking attendant'.

'Not much running where the Magician was concerned. Free walking was more his style. Running is for people with somewhere to be.'

'Free running?'

'It's a sport for crazy people,' said Rav, 'You climb a building from the outside, jumping from rooftops like a bloody monkey. And like everything else monkeys do, it's bad for your health.'

'Ah,' said Barry, his finger outstretched, 'that's the thing, though. Free runners climb buildings. Nobody ever saw the Magician climb anything. He would just end up on top of a car park, or an office rise. Sure, he would jump to other buildings, but nobody saw how he reached the top of the first one. Like with the Bullring.'

'The Bullring?' I asked.

'Big shopping centre in Birmingham. Guess what shape it is. It's where I first saw the Magician.

'I was driving vans back then, and even classy places like the Bullring need blokes to drive stuff around. Anyways, I was stretching my legs when I noticed that everyone was stopping to look up. People never look up without a reason, so I looked up as well. That's when I saw the guy.

'He looked like a Dane. Blonde hair. Face that looked like it had been carved by an ice sculptor. Maybe six-three, six-four. And he was walking on the glass canopy of the Bullring like it was a country road. Head up, looking at the sky, wandering over the panes as if he wasn't crazy. People were yelling at him, telling him to get down, and he was looking around to see if there was some other lunatic the good Brummie people were talking to. Even when the police sent a bloke to bring him down, you could see the Magician couldn't work out what he was doing wrong.'

Barry paused to pick up a chip, and took a bite out of it.

'I don't think the police could work out what he was doing wrong either, 'cause they let him go. After all, it's not trespassing if you're walking on top of a public building, is it?'

'It most definitely is,' said Rav.

Barry sighed. 'Look, don't get legal on me. You're ruining it.

'So anyway, the minute he gets away from the police, I go up to him. He looked scruffy, apart from his shoes. They were unbranded trainers, brilliant white. Unmarked. Perfectly curved around his massive feet. I say to him, "You went up on the roof, didn't you?"

'The guy thought for a bit, and said, "Hmm." Just "hmm." That was another thing about him. Quiet. I only heard him say three words. "Hmm" was the first. He didn't need to say anything. He did things. He walked. I heard he walked everywhere. Some blokes I talked to here said they saw him in Cardiff, Newcastle, Edinburgh...'

'Hang on,' I said, 'If he was that big a deal, why don't more people know about him?'

'He never did London,' said Barry, 'It's the one city he didn't do. If he did, people like me wouldn't need to talk about him.'

'If he did, people would have forgotten him a week later,' said Rav, 'He only did one trick, and that one did for him in the end.'

'A trick?' As my hunger ebbed, I was getting curious. 'What kind of trick?'

'The Flight of the Magician,' said Rav. 'His first and last.'

'You know,' said Barry, 'If the Magician were a normal person that would have been bad taste.'

'Why, what happened to him?'

'It was the last time I saw the Magician. I was in Luton. I spotted him on top of a multi-story car park – one joined up to a cinema across the way by a tube walk-way. Nobody noticed him there, so I thought I'd head up and join him.

'He was doing his usual carefree walk and I wondered, he's been all over the country, he must have picked up some kind of trick here or there. So I said to him, "Do you do stunts?"

'He didn't understand. So I tried different words. "Trick? Big Finish?" And I did this,' Barry brought his hands together, then took them apart, fingers splayed in a mini-explosion. 'The Magician seemed to understand that one. He smiled an idiotic grin. Then he said, "Wodge dis."

'He walked out on that walkway – on top of it, of course. He walked out halfway, and stopped. Then he turned to his left, one quarter turn, spread his arms and jumped.'

Barry sighed. 'For a second, I thought he was actually going to fly. It took a while for gravity to kick in, but kick it did. He plummeted – that's the only word for it. I was already bracing for the sound of his body hitting tarmac. But it didn't come – because his body never hit the ground. His clothes were there, outlining his shape in the middle of the road, but the Magician had completely disappeared.

'He's another traveller like you or me. He's on another journey now, in some distant place, looking for other rooftops.

'I wanted to keep something of the Magician. He might want his clothes back sometime. After the fall I raced down. I went as fast as I could and I didn't see anyone about, but bugger me if someone hadn't stolen his shoes.'

My gaze snapped to his feet under the table, but all I saw was a scuffed pair of boots.

About the author: Jonny Rowland might as well live in Narnia, seeing as no one knows that his hometown exists. A twenty-something graduate of the University of Warwick's post-grad writing programme, he is currently spending his time writing a novel deconstructing the superhero. As you do.

Learn more about Jonny on his blog: jonnyrowland.wordpress.com

Or follow him on Twitter: @rowland_jonny

The Changeling by Polly Robinson

'What are these things?' Sarah asks, picking up a pinch of pointy green stick-like things the size of hundreds and thousands.

John stares, his eyes wide in amazement. 'They're tiny! How on earth did you spot them?'

He's right; mortals rarely see faerie teeth.

The collective gasp from the fae sounds like a breath of wind; Alemin flies, his wings on fire, to the faerie court.

'Mortals! Mortals!' he wheezes, 'Found the teeth.'

The faerie queen grins, her mouth glittering greenly, 'Mark her! We'll take the child.'

The fae pack their string pockets. They have nectar to feed the mortal babe and keep it quiet when they put the changeling in its place. The faerie court, the tannafae, wants a blue-eyed, blonde-haired boy child to pet, cosset and tease ... to keep for the solstice. The fae hunters head for the land of mortals.

'This way.' Alemin leads as they leave the magical meadow-scented realm. They pass through the hawthorn to the world of mortals. Alemin hates the green stained teeth; he rubs a tooth-cleansing twig over his own to freshen his mouth. He hears them chattering and jittering behind him; he sees squirrels leap up trees, rabbits disappear down holes. There are snuffles and scuffles. Twigs snap. He was born into fae. Why is he different? Why can't he feel a part of them? Alemin glances up through the dappled canopy, mottled sunshine picks out bright spikily waxed hair, disproportionately large knuckled hands, thin fingers, tapered nails. He is aware of them scraping the unmistakeable fae marks in moss and on tree bark. Coal black faerie eyes glitter, the fae sneer at the creatures scattering before them.

At Alemin's raised hand the fae hunters quieten and move swiftly, silently in shoes of scuffed moleskin. Alemin carries a poor sickly little mite, blue-eyed and blonde-haired, a faerie baby, the one his family call the good-for-nothing, the changeling. He does not like it, what he is about to do, but it must be done. He, Alemin, must be elevated to the position of tannafae and from there to faepeer. He has little choice until he can win enough favour to become tannafae. They reach the archaic ridgeway and work along it. There, in front of them, appears the isolated cottage. Alemin makes a wide sweep with his arm and the fae blend into the gorse and bracken on the hillside. Not a sound is made.

Alemin sees Sarah pegging out washing. She is their target mother; the mortal who picked up the faerie teeth. Alemin and the others enter the farmworker's cottage. They snatch Sarah's child from the cradle and Alemin deposits the faerie changeling. Without a backward glance, the fae leave. Alemin stops outside the window to see what Sarah will do. She peels potatoes for dinner, cries over onions, then she moves to the cradle. Alemin sees her tilt her head to the side as if puzzled. He stiffens. Will she realise? No. Trick of the light. She tucks the blankets around the tiny child. She smiles fondly at the baby who grizzles in its sleep.

The tannafae coo over the tiny new mortal, delighted with the blue eyes and blonde hair. They pinch it to make it cry then pick it up and fuss it. Alemin sees they love the novelty. He feels sick. They chuck it under its chin to receive a gummy smile. They feed it on nectar, giggling as it becomes drunk and starts to hiccup. Alemin looks away.

The faerie queen smiles and nods her head graciously. She is pleased with Alemin.

He shivers as he thinks about the solstice, the blood-tithe. Before the last solstice he talked with his father.

'Why do we need mortal blood?'

'Because otherwise it would have to be fae blood.'

'But it is fae blood if we give away our weak and feeble to get mortals'

'That's not how she sees it. The fae hunters search for the mortals who find faerie teeth. It has been so for centuries.'

'They are away from their families for months. What's the good of that? There has to be a better way.'

'You are a great hunter, Alemin, you have the knack of spotting teeth finders and marking them for the blood-tithe.'

'But there must be a better way.'

'Find it, my son. Get into court. Become a tannafae. With good fortune you could be nominated a faeseer, then you'll make your mark.'

Alemin knows he has pleased the faerie queen. He will soon join the tannafae.

At the faerie court, the tannafae fun lasts until the babe is so hungry it won't stop crying and doesn't smile any more. They tire of sticking it with pins to make it scream louder. Now the sacrifice is made, the blood-tithe gathered. They put the limp bloodless body on the bones of others in the Northern cave; the babe will die of cold, blood poisoning and anaemia.

Another half dozen and the fae will be safe until winter solstice.

About the author: This is the second of Polly Robinson's stories in this anthology. Read more about Polly on her blog at journalread.wordpress.com

White Noise by David K. Paterson

If you are hearing this, your life is in danger. Turn off this message and destroy your computer. It's your only hope.

Still here? Okay, I'll try and convince you. Imagine a cold, winter's morning in the year 2009. The snow outside was deep and crisp and even. Yeah, right. It was slushy underfoot, the sky was grey and it'd been raining since October. It was perfect weather for a geek like me to stay indoors, watch The Guild and build the most advanced cryptographic program ever conceived. I was pushing myself to my limits and my computer even further. I'd already fried three processors from over-clocking them and still the program wouldn't run.

I looked over the result of my latest hacking marathon, certain that I'd optimised the code as much as possible. I hit the compile button and watched the green, mono-spaced letters stream across my screen. I waited, my heart pounding, eager to run this new version. Had I finally cracked it?

The scrolling stopped. 'Compilation complete. Press F9 to run.'

Oh, frakabanjo.

My finger hovered over the key. With my eyes on the screen, I pressed the button.

I remember a cloud of blue-grey smoke, because I inhaled it and spent the next day as high as a kite. The image of the exploding computer buried itself in my memory, shards of melted, black plastic embedding themselves in the walls. Being flung to the floor saved me from being sliced by the shrapnel.

I'm just proving my credentials. I know you've been there too. We're brothers in geek-hood. For the brain-scrambling stuff, we need to jump forward a couple of years to early December 2011. Your curiosity is growing, isn't it? Well, you know what they say about that and cats...

The setback didn't stop me for long. I'd never been more relieved to have a back-up of my program. I re-factored my code to within an inch of its bytes and now I was ready, my finger hovering once again over the F9 key. A little more wary, of course. I'm not suicidal. I pressed the button and beat a retreat. The computer sounded like it was attempting lift-off. I braced for another explosion, hiding my face in my hands. The wailing fans stepped up a gear. The bearings became shrieking banshees. I smelled the familiar stink of stressed circuits. I was micro-seconds from another failure.

The room fell quiet, the computer's normal hum returning. After a few seconds, I peered through my fingers and saw my stark, gun-metal grey user interface appear. I got to my feet, not entirely convinced that the computer wasn't about to blow up.

To be sure I wasn't going to make a huge fool of myself when I released the program, I had to prove that only encrypted data would be decrypted. I already knew what I wanted to use as my control. I have an old radio on when I'm working; it saves having to switch back to Twitter to find out the news. I span the dial to a random patch of static. A blast of white noise from the beginning of the universe would soon show if the code was working or not.

I made the necessary connections, piping the radio's output into my computer. I spun the dial to a random frequency, static hissing from the speakers. My program recognised that the random noise wasn't encrypted and left it well enough alone. Satisfied, I prepared to move on to the secure data tests, lining up the sample files while the white noise filled the room. And then it wasn't. Without warning, a husky, rasping voice wrapped itself around my eardrums and scoured them for a few moments until they were raw.

'Speak English, T'Rel needs the practice.' The sandpaper-smooth voice was replaced by another.

'T'Rel doesn't see why, K'Rel. Once we invade, they will all be speaking Rellian'. I leaned closer to the computer, wondering if I'd accidentally tuned the radio into some bad sci-fi show. My cryptography program continued to run, forgotten.

'Once we invade, T'Rel. Patience is the key. The humans are programmed to self-destruct. That is when we strike. When they are weak enough.'

The first voice made a dismissive, grunting noise. 'T'Rel is impatient, K'Rel.'

'What the hell ...?' I muttered, a little too close to the microphone, as it turned out.

The voices stopped. I had enough time to wonder if I'd imagined the whole thing when three slow, rasping words sent chills coursing down my spine.

'Who is that!?'

I jumped, scooting my chair away from the computer.

'Who is there? K'Rel demands an answer!'

I stood and tiptoed back, wondering whether this was the result of too many late nights and furry pizza slices. I soon had my answer.

'K'Rel said, who are you!?'

I think I screamed a little.

'Human!' the voice screamed in reply. 'T'Rel, a human has decrypted the carrier signal! Track them down and destroy them before they reveal us!'

'Yes, K'Rel, by your command.'

I crashed into my desk, the computer rocking before giving into gravity and toppling off the edge.

'Human!' the first voice roared. 'T'Rel is coming ...'

The voice cut out as the computer crashed onto the floor, the screen following close behind. A familiar acrid stink gushed out of the wrecked equipment. I sat on the floor, gulping in deep breaths of the foul fog as my heart thumped. I didn't hear that, I told myself, but I didn't believe it. I grabbed my coat and stuffed my USB key into my pocket. I knew what I needed. A grande mocha at Starbucks would put my sleep-deprived mind back on track.

'Mum? Dad? Just...' I leaned against the door, trying to control my pounding pulse and breathlessness. 'Just popping out.'

I opened the front door and stepped out into the late summer evening, bathing in the warmth of the sun. Rather too much warmth. The hairs were standing up on my arms and tiny sparks of electricity arced between them.

'What the ...?' I managed, before the world went white.

I woke up in the bushes on the other side of the street, flaming bricks, tiles and glass smashing down around me. My ears rang, the world muffled and fuzzy. A slate slammed into the grass inches from me and I flung my arms over my head, protecting myself as masonry destroyed the neighbourhood. When I next looked up, dust was drifting in the air, covering everything in a fine, white powder. I looked around at my house, or rather at the crater where my house had been. Torn water pipes spat, dribbled and poured. The gas main spouted a roaring flame. Bizarrely, the garden was still mostly intact, Dad's prize roses scorched but otherwise undamaged, Mum's greenhouse with only one broken pane of glass. There was no trace of my parents. I stumbled away in shock as the sound of sirens approached.

I've been on the run ever since. I didn't even dare to go to my parents' funerals. I'm stopping at this coffee shop to record this message, because I have to warn you. I've read about mysterious explosions around the world. I know my fellow nerds are finding the frequency and decoding the signal. I pray you believe me, because I've seen things, out of the corner of my eye, shadows that you could pass off as a trick of the light. They said I was paranoid. Well, just because you're paranoid doesn't mean they aren't out to get you, does it? They won't ever stop and I know my time is running out. If you continue with your work, they'll come for you too. So, for the last time, do as I ask. Turn off this recording and destroy your computer, before it's too la...

About the author: David K. Paterson is a dreamer, geek and aspiring author; a powerful combination in the right hands! David's journey as a writer is just beginning and he can't wait to see where it takes him.

Follow David on Twitter at @thedkpaterson

Other Things by Thomas Pitts

The last stars are bleaching out in the pre-dawn. Through the missing pane - removed to make the house appear unoccupied - he gazes at the grey silhouettes of the little wind turbines. On the roofs of the street they fit awkwardly.

'Honey,' whispers his wife up the stairs, 'does it look safe?'

You can hear everything in this quiet world now. He goes down.

His wife hands him his backpack. 'No rats in the traps. And the rainwater's still too toxic for growing. Look at her.' - Their four-year-old. 'Our priority's food. Don't go searching for other things till you've gotten us something to eat.'

Checking his weapons - spear (from a broom handle), shriekgun, and meat cleaver - he says, 'You talk like it was all my fault. I'm a mathematician. I wasn't an economist or a businessman, or a politician.'

Then his sunglasses and waterproof. His wife inspects him for bare skin.

'Don't take short cuts through dangerous neighbourhoods.'

'And come back,' says his daughter meekly. She's a sickly child, and covered in blotches.

He hugs her. 'I'll bring you back something good to eat. While I'm away you can go through your alphabet with Mommy.' Avoiding the frown on his wife's lean face, he goes to the yard door. 'Literacy will be useful for leaving messages and such.'

He nods goodbye and goes across the backyard and into the neighbour's yard, and begins along the whole street of overgrown gardens. He glances, as usual, at the shallow graves in Mrs Ramirez' flowerbed. How many had they buried there?

Non-native flower species transported from half a world away.

Ships. Airplanes.

Not long ago - not long ago at all - you couldn't look up without seeing an airliner. He determines again not to allow the past to fade into legend. He mustn't become preoccupied only with foraging for food, with basic necessities. A human can't live on such things alone.

As he goes through the gap in Mr Sangha's hedge, he recalls the Mars landings. For the public it had been a contemptible waste of resources, but for him it was a spiritual experience. Humankind had escaped to a new planet, if only for a few months. That had to mean something.

He looks up. Twisters in the south.

Oakland's flooded.

And westward is all gangland.

That leaves the Doglands, where feral canines have grown big on human corpses.

He looks at the sun: already mid-morning. Turning north, he unshoulders the spear. Save the gun's charge for human enemies.

Wolf-like muzzles look up from their snouting to watch him go by. He makes himself look big, but one scabby monster comes up growling. He levels his spear at it. Keeping the point there, he picks up and throws some heavy object: the dog cowers. (A mail-order catalogue.) But other dogs come up and reinforce their leader. Too many for the cleaver - he might get bitten. He discharges the shriekgun. It does the trick, sending them away whining like they're only pets after all. He marches on.

In priority order:

Food.

Aspirin.

Footwear.

Sunscreen.

Water-purifying tablets.

Charger for the energy rifle.

Any medicine.

Since he's in the Doglands: how far is his old workplace? Surely not so far - a slight detour is all. He might find something useful that direction.

It's farther than he remembers - he had never walked to work. But anyhow, here's a pharmacy.

It's gutted, not only of medicine, but of anything the gangs can use to escape reality or to trade for food.

He turns the corner into College Ave. Here's the old building. The 'E' has fallen off, so now the letters stand for Search for Terrestrial Intelligence. The world is so full of ironies nowadays this one barely registers. The building has suffered only superficial damage, so that as he nears it he can easily imagine himself coming in for a shift. How pleasant life had been. Intensely *pleasant*. How civilized - the work atmosphere, the reassuring machine noises, the jokes with your workmates - folk who'd shared the same commitment to an interesting, important enterprise.

The entrance has done its job, hastily erected though it was during the Rioting. The rioters had targeted science indiscriminately but if science and technology had limited itself to such as SETI...The ultracarbon of the Identifier is heavily scarred where someone's tried to shoot a way in, but it looks essentially undam-

The entrance opens.

It must recognize him. He doesn't move.

Inside is the past.

He glances at the sun: nearly midday. What should he do?

Maybe he'll find the charger he needs? He realizes he is entering inside.

The entrance closes and on comes the lighting around him - some of the solar roof tiling must be functioning. The place is unchanged since the day the boss told everyone to go home to their families.

Familiar machine noises. Bringing back the feeling of-☐

A movement! He drops down and fumbles out the shriekgun.

It's just a cleanerbot - amazingly still doing its job. He waits for his heart to become inaudible again. Strange that you care so much about survival when life isn't worth living.

He decides to commence a search of the entire building. He passes through:

Offices.

Canteens.

Corridors.

Stairwells.

On untidy desks are scraps of paper. Calculations of signal strengths, schematic sketches of areas of the Galaxy, a list of frequencies - not all of them ticked off. The writing is small so as to conserve paper, and yet someone had drawn a cartoon of

ET. Everything is as it was left on that last day of work. He becomes increasingly surprised not to come across his old workmates. Someone should finish off that list of frequencies. It seems a contradiction.

Remembering that daylight dictates things now, he hurries through the remainder of the building. He takes the soap from the bathroom. Antibac-antifungal.

On the way out he stops at his old workstation. It seems so much more convincing than everything outside…He winks at the unit. That little tune as on it comes! And the slow whirl of old data!…If only he was analyzing that now, losing himself in otherworldly labours…

Wait, this data is current…Hmph, so that's the date. One of the receiver stations is still functioning and relaying…That would be something, if aliens have been discovered and are coming to the rescue. He has to leave.

Instead he stands there gazing into the data-swirl. In all the broken world, here is the loveliest thing. Had it mattered that SETI had discovered no intelligent life? It had been the expectation that had made it so meaningful.

An unfamiliar icon is flashing…Priority red. Responding to his stare, it enlarges and explains itself.

Non-natural signal discovered.

His eyes unfocus. Unable to speak, he manipulates the data literally, fumblingly.

The signal was recorded…four years ago, on 9-19-2040.

Then he remembers that the confirmatory test always delivered *False reading*. He runs the test. So many falses over the years, you just don't expect confirmation.

No false readings.

His pulse accelerates. What next? ...The full confirmatory program. He runs it.

...

No false readings.

After some time his mouth croaks the question, 'Is this intelligent life?'

The unit talks slowly. 'It sure is.'

His head seems full only of some light element, like ozone, like he might float.

'Location-of-source,' he says at last.

'Rho Coronae Borealis.'

Fifty-five light years. So near!

What's next? What do you do next? What's the procedure? The signal pattern is complex, very complex, as complex as civilization.

'Is it meaningful?'

'The message is in sixty-eight languages.'

His mind won't move. At last, he asks, 'Earth languages?'

'Uh-huh.'

'Symbolic or mathematical languages?'

'Regular verbal languages.'

'They must have translated our languages.' He hears himself ask, 'When was it sent?'

'June twenty 1985.'

'Of course…Read it - in English. Let me sit down first!'

The chair forms intelligently around him. But for some reason he isn't comfortable, can't get comfortable. At last he just has to nod 'Go ahead.'

The pause of a second seems to last a minute. He isn't breathing right.

The message begins.

'To planet Earth, in truth, beauty, and goodness, from the people of planet Athyre: greetings. The radio signals from your planet are of interest. We have dispatched a diplomatic mission to arrive (your date) October 2111. We advise you of ourselves as follows. Our planet…'

The message continues but now the words, English though they are, are staying as pure sounds, which his brain won't convert into meaning. There's some kind of other noise going on in his head. He can't concentrate, just *can't get the sounds into words* - it's just *sounds* or barks he's hearing now.

Why is he thinking of food?

The dogs are barking at the entrance.

Food.

Aspirin.

Footwear.

Medicine.

Sunscreen.

Water-purifying tablets.

About the author: Thomas Pitts (born 1983) is half Italian and lives in Newbury, Berkshire. He has had two mainstream short stories broadcast on BBC Radio 4 and is just completing a science fiction novel.

Beyond the fringe by Natalie Kleinman

The pattern on the carpet drifted as I watched. The familiar lines and colours moved apart and reformed into something unknown; alien. It occurred to me that I might be hallucinating but as I hadn't smoked anything, hadn't drunk anything or popped any pills, I dismissed these as the cause of my predicament. Predicament? Hardly an adequate word for whatever was happening. I tried to look away but I was mesmerised. The carpet, measuring about six feet by four, raised itself from the floor. Omigod! One minute I'm sitting reading a book, minding my own business and the next I'm up in the air; me who likes to have her feet firmly on the ground. I was paralysed with fear, all except my gut which was churning like a food processor.

I looked in astonishment at the gold, green and red fringes around the edge of the rug where once had been a smooth finish. Not only that, the colour scheme was completely different from the one I'd chosen with such care only a few weeks before. Indignation crept in amongst my other emotions; as if I didn't have enough to worry about. This rug no longer matched the décor. It was beginning to look like I was on some sort of trip after all.

I had nothing to grab onto as I was lifted into space in defiance of gravity, but somehow balance wasn't a problem. I stayed safely in the centre, feeling no motion (though plenty of emotion) but knowing I was moving. The gentle breeze, increasing in strength, wafted my hair away from my face. The walls of my sitting room receded in a blur taking the ceiling with them and I found myself carried upwards into fading light. I tried before it was too late to exit my odd mode of transport. I dived for the edge, knocking the book aside in my scramble, but banged into an invisible barrier. The book rebounded and landed cover up on the rug displaying its title: In the Ascendancy. My imagination went into overdrive; a force field? Impossible, but then so was the fact that I was no longer sitting in my own home. Even without the barrier it would have been suicide to jump off as by now I was too high to see the ground beneath. Soon the light had vanished completely and though I've never been afraid of the dark this was different. Primeval fear swamped me as a rush of adrenalin left me gasping for air.

I shivered but it wasn't from cold. It struck me as odd that there was no change in temperature, no awareness of the elements. Then I laughed hysterically as I realised this was perhaps the least odd thing about the whole experience. Much stranger was the fact that I had been taken out of my environment, out of my world, and was on a journey to who knew where. Normally the hairs on my arms only react to cold but now they were on full alert, standing to attention.

The lights came on suddenly and I found myself, still on the carpet, on the rim of a large circle with others, each on their own rug, all the same pattern, all with those awful fringes, and every one looking as bewildered as I felt. The circle wasn't hung in space either. We were stationary now on a firm annular base, most definitely not my sitting room floor. It stretched outwards for some feet until it met a wall that rose all the way round to form a dome above our heads. I had no idea how we'd entered the dome. There was no opening, no visible gateway. By this time normal had ceased to apply. My memories of early Star Trek episodes left me believing it was possible to be transported from one place to another by means outside accepted parameters. "Beam me up, Scottie" no longer seemed such a strange concept. I looked around at my companions. We were a pretty mixed bunch. There was an elderly wheelchair-bound lady looking absolutely stunned –

and who could blame her? A young mother was kneeling on her rug, caught in the act of changing her baby's nappy. An almost-finished jigsaw puzzle on a large white board took centre stage on another, the woven threads a startling background for the tranquil chocolate-box scene. The human occupant sat staring, open-mouthed, a piece of the jigsaw in her hand and looking as if this was one puzzle she wasn't going to be able to solve. I counted twelve in all including myself, evenly spaced, and I was struck by our resemblance to the numbers on a clock face.

Intuition told me we'd arrived simultaneously. Maybe it was the suspended motion of the puzzler or the mother so obviously in the act of removing the used nappy. I put my hand out towards the centre of the dome, expecting the same invisible obstruction I'd experienced before. It wasn't there. I rose to my feet and moved to the middle of the space. Others too leapt into action. I realised we were all women, except for the baby who proved he was a boy by sending a stream of wee into the air, his mother's practised hand blocking it immediately with a clean piece of gauze.

'I'm Rose,' she announced rather too loudly. It was enough.

'So am I.'

'Me too.'

'And me.'

Odd. Decidedly odd; but then everything was odd, wasn't it?

'Rose Cavendish.' she spoke again.

'Now that's weird,' said the puzzle lady.

'You're not kidding,' I said. '*I'm* Rose Cavendish.'

By now surreal just wasn't in it. This was no dream, but it didn't exactly feel like reality either. Rose, the mother, picked up her son and patted his back for comfort, but for whose comfort I wasn't sure. The child looked perfectly at ease so I guess it was hers. Rose with grey hair and all the apparent authority of her age wheeled her chair to take centre stage just as a loud hum began and a cylinder descended from the middle of the ceiling. Her hearing aid evidently wasn't that efficient because she didn't look up and I sprung forward to push her out of the way. The bottom of the cylinder made contact with the floor and I swung the wheelchair round to face it. A door slid open. Adam stepped out.

'*Adam!*' I began to tremble. I'd coped fairly well, I thought, with the events that had begun with my carpet ride and, apart from a very natural stupefaction, almost taken them in my stride; but *ADAM?*

He took my hands in his.

'I can explain.'

'That would be good. It had better be good.'

I sensed rather than saw the question in the faces of every other Rose in the dome.

'You look beautiful. You've no idea how I've longed for this moment. It's been years, Rose.'

'It's been twenty-four hours, and you didn't come home last night.'

'I've been travelling, Rose; travelling in time; in space. I've been away for nearly three hundred years.'

'Of course you have. And you don't look a day older than you did yesterday. And why are we here? Why all these other Roses?' Okay, perhaps my voice rose by a few decibels but stress does that to you; stress and anger.

'Two reasons, Rosie. If I'd come straight back to Frankston you'd never have believed me.'

'Whatever gave you that idea?' I'm not above a little sarcasm either.

'The other reason is a bit more complicated. I've seen things that would blow your mind; learned about stuff we've only imagined back on Earth, it isn't always straightforward. Odd things happen in space and time. I was never a believer in little green men and I've seen nothing to make me change my mind; but there are other entities out there, Rose, far more intelligent than ours. There are light years between us – literally. I've come back as an emissary; with evidence. I want you to be part of it. I had to make sure I got back to the right Rose Cavendish. You see, it wasn't quite as simple as just landing in the sitting room. I had to summon up every Rose Cavendish within a radius of twenty miles and I really didn't think there'd be so many of you.'

He made it sound like an accusation; like it was our fault.

'Okay, we're all here now. You've got the right Rose, along with several others. So tell me; how do we get home?'

Adam appeared rather uncomfortable as he looked around at the assembled Roses.

'That's the problem,' he said. 'I'm afraid I don't know.'

About the author: Natalie Kleinman has been writing for about ten years. Having successfully broken into the short story market her first novel is now nearing completion. She took up writing in the mistaken belief this would be a gentle pursuit. It didn't take long for it to become an intense passion.

Dorothy by Dawn Hudd

Dorothy worshipped technology. Literally. The Great Web had spoken to her six months previously when she was checking her emails. The message came to her indirectly through an angel called Kesha Rains. The subject line read 'life enhancing change' and when she opened it the page was covered in a mass of jumbled up words and disjointed letters. Dorothy was about to delete it when right in the centre of the page she saw the words 'Great Web' – a message from the Master Himself. Two weeks later she had deciphered the message.

She didn't tell anyone about the Great Web. You are chosen, the message said. Well actually, the message was *you be chose* but she wasn't about to worry about grammar and punctuation. 'No-one tell of the Great Web' she read. So she waited.

Dorothy discovered technology rather late in life. Sean, her only son, decided to emigrate to the other side of the world in order to make a 'better life' for his family. That life was a large house with swimming pool and Christmas barbeques, and, ultimately, a divorce when his wife ran off leaving Sean with their two young children. Before he left for Sydney he purchased the best computer he could afford, set up a broadband connection, and installed it in Dorothy's front room.

Email was a godsend. Sean sent photos of the children regularly and they talked on the phone. Dorothy, retired and on her own since Reg died, could sit up until the early hours and chat away when it was mid-afternoon for them. The kids weren't cranky or tired and were always pleased to talk to Granny in England. At times like that Sydney didn't seem so far away.

Dorothy had been sixty-two when Sean had left. Since then she'd worked her way around email, joined online communities where she discussed knitting techniques, and ordered her weekly shopping online. This machine, which frightened her at first, was now part of her family. It was her closest friend. She told her doctor so at her annual check-up and noticed his indulgent smile and additional notes in her file. So what if he thought she was a senile old codger? She still went out to her bridge club every week, though that was getting smaller as her friends dropped dead one by one. You could do anything on a PC these days and for the time when the bridge club disappeared, Dorothy had already sussed a few online clubs.

Sean's divorce coincided with the message from the Great Web. Sean soon sent a heartfelt plea for Dorothy to join him in Sydney as 'the kids need a Gran'. More likely he missed having someone to run around after them. Unfortunately for Sean, his plea also coincided with Dorothy's translation of the message, which told her most assuredly (Dot do not dash) not to go. 'I'm too old to go chasing off to the other side of the world', she told him.

Dorothy spent more time in front of the computer screen in the month before the Ascension, as she came to call it. She discovered VOIP – Voice Over Internet Protocol. It meant that she could talk to Sean for free, and with a camera as well she could see the children.

Sean looked haggard, but Dorothy stuck firm to the Great Web's instructions. Two weeks before the Ascension, Sean found himself a lady friend. Gail was a sweet looking girl, if a bit bleach-blonde, but the children liked her. Sean spoke highly of her and that was what mattered.

In the final weeks messages and signs from the Great Web were more frequent. This amused Dorothy. She'd always considered herself an atheist, obstinately denying the possibility of the existence of any kind of God. She suffered festivals such as Easter and Christmas purely for the children. Now here she was, worshipping a greater being.

The messages, from Shake Nairs or Kansas Hire, could be small or large, but they always needed decoding, and were often quite oblique. The message remained, though. Tell no-one. Keep the faith.

One Wednesday her shopping didn't arrive. Then she realised she hadn't actually ordered anything. She chastised herself for her forgetfulness. What would the Great Web think? The computer was there to be used for the greater good, and recently the Great Web had sent her an article on how the internet provided jobs for thousands of people through e-commerce. The market place was booming, it said, and Dorothy was pleased with herself for being part of that growth. For a while she felt that she'd let Him down, but made up for her shortfall by ordering flowers for Gail, sent direct to Australia, and some wines for Sean. She also ordered some Lucky Dip sacks for the children from a major toy shop. She felt somehow vindicated in the screen of the Great Web.

Dorothy wanted to bring herself closer to Him, so she studied some of the world's great religions. One of the common features in many of these religions was some sort of altar involving light. Dorothy knew that naked flames and electrical equipment didn't mix, so she bought herself a lava lamp that plugged directly into the PC to illuminate the portal. In the darkness it glowed comfortingly. Dorothy didn't turn the computer off at all now since she had moved her bed into the living room. It would have been a sin to move the PC upstairs. Here it was in its rightful place. In the final weeks, whenever a message came from Himself the lava lamp showed a great flurry of activity.

Dorothy felt excitement bubbling deep inside. The time was near. She didn't know what would happen, but she prayed it would be when the people of the world would come to know the Great Web for themselves.

Soon there was an email every day, from Sienna Shark, Sean Ark His or Saran Sheik. She was adept at decoding now and the messages were more specific. Be ready. Be prepared. The time is soon.

Dorothy was tired. She had been talking to Sean for more than hour. He was bright and chirpy, but it was mid afternoon for him. For Dorothy it was the middle of the night, and she couldn't remember the last time she had eaten. She said goodbye and slipped into the kitchen for warm milk. Her head felt fuzzy.

She couldn't resist a final check before she slept. She opened her email. Her heart leapt when she saw the sender. Nasa Shrike! It was He! This time it had an attachment. Tentatively she clicked on the paperclip. There was only word in the document.

NOW

Dorothy clutched at her chest. The pain was brief and excruciating.

She let herself be led into the garden. It was beautiful. No-one spoke, but she knew it was OK. She was with Him. She could feel His presence all around. She was among friends. She was the Chosen One.

It was her neighbour who found her sitting there, smiling but stone cold. Sean was devastated. 'She didn't suffer,' the doctor assured him.

Sean flew back to England alone. Looking around his mother's living room he berated himself for not realising sooner how hard she had been finding things. The bed in the living room was a dead giveaway. Dorothy had angled the webcam so that he hadn't been able to see the changes she had made, but it was obvious she hadn't been coping.

The man from the auction house told Sean he would get a tidy sum for the couple of antiques in the house. The funeral was a quiet affair, with only the three members of her bridge club, now disbanded, Dorothy's GP, the shopping delivery driver, and Sean. Very soon he was back in Sydney, a slightly richer man.

Sean couldn't sleep. He turned on his computer. It was strange. For years he had talked to Dorothy on it, but now she was gone. He went to his inbox. Blast. His spam filter was letting him down. There was some mail that was obviously junk. It had to be, with a sender called Aries Shank. He went to hit delete but stopped. He *wanted* to open it. He felt compelled to click on the subject line – 'she new now' – regardless of the risks. There was no message, but there *was* an attachment. He clicked on the little paperclip and the screen blacked out.

He cursed. A virus! Almost immediately the red light on his webcam flickered. The screen blinked back to life. Sean felt his mouth drop open as he stared at the image beginning to form.

About the author: Dawn Hudd is a writer and teacher from the West Midlands. She shares her home with her family and other animals. Dawn has had a number of short stories published in anthologies.

Human Fossil by Denise Hayes

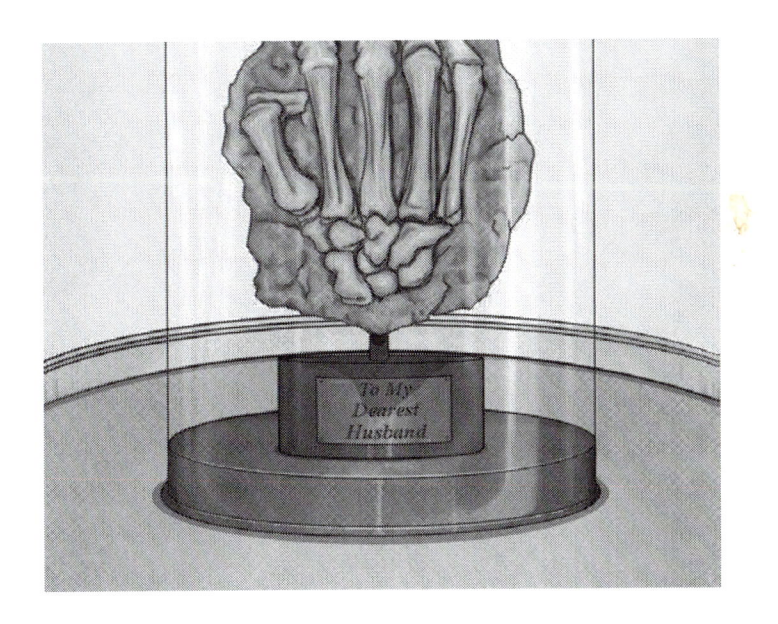

When Sven first suggested that Galatea become a human fossil she had some misgivings. She had accepted that her heart was broken beyond repair (even had the guarantee not run out) but she still couldn't quite contemplate yet the reality of her imminent death.

Sven told her often how inconsolable he was that within a very short time he would no longer enjoy her physical presence. He'd invested much of his family inheritance in the medical fees needed to sculpt Galatea's body and face to the degree of perfection he sought. Most recently each breast had cost the equivalent of one year's salary tokens. The very thought that her beautifully pert upturned nose and her permanently plumped lips would soon succumb to the processes of decay and putrefaction was enough to send him into a diatribe of blame and complaint. He was angry with the medics who tried to say it was the countless operations that had ultimately weakened and then destroyed Galatea's organic heart.

'If only you'd kept up with the exercise program I devised,' he'd said on receipt of the *Terminal Notification*, 'we could've got years yet out of your body.'

So when Sven spotted the advert from the South Dakota Human Fossil Company he leapt at the chance to preserve Galatea's beauty forever. He sat Galatea in front of his computer screen, 'See – read that. If you like, you can choose your own stratum.'

The advert read:

Want to live forever? Want to leave your imprint?
The South Dakota Human Fossil Company's patented petrification process can immortalise your entire body (or - at a reduced rate - selected body parts) within the geological stratum of your choice. Take our online virtual tour of geographical locations, geological time periods and petrification packages.

The details of the actual process were a little grim and Galatea couldn't help but think that an instantaneous transformation to a pile of dust in the incineration centres was somehow more decorous and more pleasingly decisive. But as she read on and researched the various time periods on offer she began to see the attraction of bedding down amongst long-lost flora and fauna.

The Pre-Cambrian period of volcano-plumed skies and quick-silver lightning had a certain apocalyptic grandeur. Galatea could imagine herself sinking into the teeming soup of primordial oceans and finding her place within silted layers of jelly fish and leaf-like sea pens.

On the other hand the Silurian strata, home to sea urchins, sea lilies and velvet worms offered more lively company. She could leave her mark in perilous times of water scorpions and sharp-jawed fish. Over the long centuries she'd toughen up with hardy brachiopods and gaze into the virgin eyes of trilobites.

It was so hard to decide. She could choose to arrive with the first bird-song or to rest by the claws of Tyrannosaurus Rex. Sven had the funds to allow her to become part of the Cretaceous outburst of flowers. A more impressive tribute than a coffin wreath, perhaps.

In the end, though, she was tempted most by the glittering aeons of the Carboniferous period – a sparkling time of giant dragonflies, silverfish and ebony-jacketed beetles.

Her decision was made.

She would leave her imprint in sea-crushed forests of club mosses, horsetails and tree-ferns.

The only question that remained was how much of her should be preserved. Sven, of course, wanted total-body transformation. Galatea was less certain. It seemed somehow wrong to leave such an unnatural body in those petrified dells. She decided to make the arrangements herself as 'a surprise' for Sven.

For the first time in many years Galatea found herself in control of what happened to her own body. Secretly she reserved a spot for her head in carboniferous strata in the Canadian Arctic. No one would ever be able to find her there. She was happy to let her silicone-implanted breasts be discarded along with her tucked and lifted buttocks. Other portions of her that had been trimmed or tightened were similarly consigned to the disposable category. One part and one part alone was to remain accessible to Sven as a final message in stone.

It didn't take Sven long after Galatea's death to line up another candidate for his care. In fact, when the message inviting him to a pre-lodgement viewing of her fossil finally arrived from South Dakota, he found it hard to fit the visit into the medical schedule he'd arranged for his new partner (it was important for him to be present at all procedures to ensure his requirements were met exactly).

He was impressed by the glossy and high-tech premises of the Human Fossil Company and his expectations were high. A slim and attractive female in a pseudo-medical uniform escorted him to the viewing chamber. 'You do understand,' she informed him with professional briskness, 'that once the fossil is embedded, additional and quite substantial funds would be required to arrange for its re-exposure. In centuries to come, of course, future geologists and archaeologists may well discover it in all its beauty.'

'Yes, yes – I understand. It's enough to know that the body is preserved.'

'Well, yes. Part of it anyway. Perhaps you'd better see for yourself.'

In the centre of the viewing chamber was a circular platform covered by a glass dome. At first there seemed to be nothing below the dome. As Sven drew closer he could see what looked to be a small lump of stone. He peered through the glass.

'Is that it? One hand?'

'Yes. It's as the subject specified. She asked for *this* item to be situated in the Pliocene period. The time when hominids – great apes - first appeared.'

Galatea's fist was clenched. But one finger pointed upwards.

Sven frowned. Galatea had told him she was leaving him a sign. Perhaps she was pointing the way ahead for him – to a new future. Maybe the sign meant she would guide him until he finally followed her. Then he noticed that the finger held aloft was not the index finger but the second one.

About the author: Denise Hayes teaches at Newman University College, Birmingham, UK. This is the second of two of her stories published in this anthology.

Golf Planet by Peter Ford

What a way to spend our eightieth wedding anniversary. On a mid-career sabbatical out here on Royal Lytham Two, seventy thousand light years from Earth. A few magical weeks on one of the great golfing planets with its low gravity and clean air.

Golf's golf though, wherever you go. Ready for that universal thwack merging into a hiss as the ball shoots away, I was about to tee off when Samine held up her hand.

'Hold it, Dan!'

I put my stroke on hold; a second more and I'd have fluffed my shot. Then came a faint rush and pull from above. I lowered my club and looked up to see one of the incoming shuttles pass overhead, full of eager golfers with their bags full of complimentary balls from the orbital station. Clubs rattled and our hair stood on end in the magnetic field. When the shiny disc had hummed down behind the ninth green centre's silver tower, I acknowledged Samine's warning and addressed the ball again for a perfect swing and follow-through. The ball compressed, its hardened silicon springing back to shape in a microsecond. Then off it went, whistling even in this light atmosphere.

I'd used a three wood for lift and we watched the shot arc up from the ridge, a dot against the pale mauve sky before it disappeared onto the green fairway winding away across red rocky desert a thousand feet below. Artificial water hazards gleamed at intervals out on the plain. The seeker light started winking on my wristset and I waited for Sam to take her shot. I admired her elegant stance as she addressed the ball. In her white cat suit with that silver blonde urchin cut she looked like a girl of fifty. Thwack and hiss again. We exchanged nods and adjusted our sets to finder mode.

'Two good ones there. We'd better get moving.'

A full kilometre drive's a good average on this low-gravity thin aired world, so we'd have some way to go. Like Gleneagles One and all these small planets, RL Two's night came quickly and our seekers were only accurate to thirty metres or so. We battened clubs onto the electric quad bikes and took a quick puff of oxygen from our inhalers. Then we were off at speed down a zigzag cliff path on our long trek to the green. Leaving the ninth tee facility far above us we looked toward the high flashing beacon marking the putting complex several kilometres away on the horizon. The rock-strewn path levelled out and we came to the fairway, a thirty metre wide path of synthetic turf stretching ahead in a gentle left-hand curve.

We drove the quads hard. The solar batteries filled easily under Lytham's white sun but we didn't want to be stuck out in the desert rough after dark, so we churned on over springy turf looking for the balls.

Mine was still on the fairway, perfectly placed for a three iron shot, and it duly disappeared with a swish toward the close horizon. Sam's had gone further into a scrabble of sharp pebbles. Warnings about straying into the rough were blazoned everywhere. Clients' own risk. As we approached, something scuttled out of sight among the rocks. We stepped gingerly onto coarse sand, alert for the feel of anything burrowing beneath our feet. Sam's ball lay in a shallow pit some ten metres from the fairway. Not as bad as the craters you get on some planets

An easy chip shot back onto the turf with a number eight and we were on the quads again, following the balls with the beepers. Three more trouble-free shots, each over a quarter of a mile and all on the fairway. And then, dazzled by the sun, I hooked my ball to the left into a small lake among low red dunes. The lake was shallow but neither of us relished the thought of wading in – especially with the warning signs. I dropped a new ball at the water's edge, adding a forfeit to my card, but before I could take my shot another ball hissed through the thin air from our right and splashed into the water.

'Whose is that?' said Samine.

'The ball you see is mine.'

A tall man jogged from behind a dune. His white hooded robe and trainers were outlandish even for a sporting world; the club in his hand even more so. Standard golf grip but with a curved back edge to the head like a small scimitar.

'I'm afraid you're wrong. See – Penfold Universal number five.'

'So's mine.'

'You can prove that by dredging it out of the pond.'

'This is the only proof I need.' He changed hands, bringing the shining blade to the fore and brandished it with a figure-eight movement.

Samine whispered, 'Dan, let him have the bloody ball. I want to walk out of here – preferably with you.'

'Well spoken, madam.' The man turned to her with a cursory bow. Then to me, 'Halves, yes?'

We don't see many scimitars in the boardroom. I nodded.

He bowed again and the weapon flashed. There on the gritty sand lay my ball in two solid silicon halves, each displaying its white outer casing and grey core. With a flourish, the man reversed his scimitar and conjured two bright new balls from a leather pouch in his white folds.

He picked up one discarded half, gesturing for me to do the same.

'For recycling,' he said, showing fine white teeth. I saw Sam relax and felt myself breathe more easily. Our new companion's short dark hair and sunburnt aquiline features marked him as a man used to the desert

'Now – coffee.' Smiling broadly he raised a finger and disappeared behind his dune, returning with a rugged two-wheeled trolley laden with various canvas sacks and a golf bag open revealing only three clubs. From a zipped compartment he produced a gas lighter and a small spirit stove with built in kettle, which he set up on the sand.

'At home, it's our tradition that once you've shared coffee you can't fall out or fight,' he explained as the stove purred.

'Pity we didn't have coffee first, then,' murmured Samine.

'Ah, that was all for show,' he said. 'Some of these golf worlders will fight to the death over whose ball it is. That can hold up your game for years while the lawyers thrash it out.'

Lytham Two is fairly mild as golf worlds go, and I hadn't expected to meet any of these fanatical types here. We were keen, but not keen enough to go golfing round eighteen planets for decades. After this trip, I thought, Lancaster will suit me fine with its haunted clubhouse and that view across the River Lune. Besides, with a hole-in-one out here I might end up buying drinks for the whole galaxy. But coffee was bubbling, the man poured three stainless steel cups and we sat round the stove. I gave our names and asked his.

'Zayed,' he replied. 'A good Earth name. Skies here are like Arabia, don't you think?'

There we both were, light years out in the universe and we'd never been to Arabia. Come to think of it, there must be space pilots who've never been to Widnes. Some of the constellations were starting to show in the darkening sky; stars familiar on Earth seen here from a different direction. In that desert, away from the clubhouse with night coming on, I felt different - vulnerable.

'We're booked in at the ninth green tonight so we'd better stop play,' I said. Lytham Two's sun was low in the sky and I reckoned we could just about make it to the complex with its roof and beds. Otherwise we'd have to set marker beacons and ride out again in the morning.

'Camp here with me,' Zayed said. 'I've a protective wire. You two have my tent and I'll sleep outside.'

'But what about the things in the sand?' Sam didn't sound too sure.

'Oh, you get snuffles and scratting but that's all. They tell you these things to keep you in the hotels. Money.'

Darkness was closing in faster than I'd expected. To continue would have been foolhardy, so an experience not offered in the brochures was our only real option.

A nod from Samine decided it. I called to tell someone in that distant beacon that we wouldn't be in.

'Are you sure that's wise, Sir? '

'We'll be fine. See you tomorrow.'

'May we have your position, Sir, in case you need us?'

'Yes, of . . .'

The handset died and I cursed myself for not leaving it in the sun to recharge. Now we really were on our own. Zayed had set up the tent and unrolled a thin wire around our campsite. His bedroll, more substantial than our thermal polybags, was laid out ready on the fairway.

While we were finishing our coffee, a silver craft from the complex swished overhead through the indigo dusk on its way to orbit. As we prepared for our first night in the open under alien stars, its receding lights seemed very far away.

About the author: Peter Ford is a retired teacher who has been reading and watching science fiction since 1947. He has had items published in various poetry anthologies, specialist journals and local newspapers.

The Meeting at the Centre of the Universe
by Walt Pilcher

Nobody is sure where the idea came from, but it was clearly time for a summit meeting of all civilizations.

The call went out on a Friday so everyone would have the weekend to think about it and plan how to use the following weeks to prepare. That is, it was a Friday on Earth, but it didn't really matter since the Earth calendar had long since been adopted as universal, modified only as necessary to accommodate differences in planetary rotation cycles and speeds of circumnavigation around suns in all the various worlds where it applied. So it was Universal Friday.

Most civilizations had the technology to traverse multiple-light-year distances in anywhere from instantaneously to no more than a day or two. Some had star drives, some had harnessed wormholes or could create and use them at will, and some could project themselves and their luggage holographically over great distances and then use local atomic material at the destination to reconstitute themselves as tangible objects or beings. Others had learned how to magnify greatly the effects of transporter technology originally developed for relatively short distances. Civilizations who hadn't achieved star travel were encouraged to hitch rides with those who had. The call invited even those worlds who had so far remained hidden and unknown, whether by choice or by oversight, to come join the convocation.

It would be the first annual summit meeting of all the vast multitudes of federations, leagues, empires, coalitions, republics, kingdoms, dictatorships, hegemonies, solar systems, and planets, both natural and artificial.

Of course, there was only one place that made sense for the meeting to be held – The Center of the Universe. That way, no favouritism would be shown or implied by holding it close to this civilization or to that one. And no one would be more or less inconvenienced by the distance than anyone else, although distance hardly mattered to most.

Such a crowd would require a large venue, even if each delegation was limited to three representatives, two transformation engineers, and a small retinue . The Universe is big – infinite in fact – so surely such a place could be found almost anywhere, and especially at the center. Unless the center was a black hole. But nobody believed it was. That was just an ancient 21st Century superstition.

Upon arrival at the center, the delegations would identify a suitable venue close enough to be declared the center for all practical purposes, and the engineers would quickly create and outfit a facility using conventional energy/matter transformation devices.

The first annual Universal Summit Meeting was now just three weeks away.

Among the agenda items:

Stabilization of exchange rates between the Uni and local currencies

Amnesty for third world aliens

Legalization of marijuana for medical purposes

Universal warming

Feverish preparations. Urgent messages back and forth. Hurried consultations. Agreements on protocol. Intense studying of the issues by the delegates, last minute instructions from their governments, and fine tuning of diplomacy training for retinue staff.

Relentlessly, the day for departure approached. Starships were outfitted. Wormhole calibrations were tweaked. Universal language translators were updated. Projectors and transporters were tested and polished, with new and redundant parts installed in fail-safe systems. Rendezvous arrangements were made.

A Universal Thursday was the agreed departure date for everyone to begin the journey from home worlds to the Summit venue.

Universal Sunday was to be the big welcoming banquet, followed on Monday by a brief opening plenary session. The remainder of the week would see a full schedule of committee meetings, subcommittee meetings, workshops, presentations of papers, debates, writing and submission of resolutions and motions, and communication back to the home worlds for reaction and further instructions, all culminating in a second plenary session on Saturday for formal arguments. The next Universal Sunday would be a day of rest and recreation, maybe time for some sightseeing at the Center of the Universe, and then on Monday final preparations would be made for voting in the closing plenary session on Tuesday. Almost two Universal Weeks in all.

Finally, it was time to go. The travellers entered their ships or mounted their pads or stood before their star gates.

The simple command was given. 'Take us to the Center!'

And nothing happened.

Anxious moments. Angry stares. Frenzied double and triple checking of equipment. Calls from civilization to civilization: 'What's going on?' 'We'll be late; don't start without us!' 'What, are you stuck too?'

Until somebody – a seminary student in a backwater solar system at the edge of one of the smaller galaxies – realized the truth: If the Universe is infinite, then every point is the center.

And that means everybody was already there. At the Center of the Universe.

Next year's meeting will be held on Rigel IV.

About the author: Walt Pilcher lives in Greensboro, NC (USA), with his wife, Carol, an artist. During his apparel industry career he moonlighted as a fiction writer, later adding poetry and songwriting with pieces appearing in a range of publications. He divides his time between family (six grandchildren), church, writing, golf and learning guitar.

Afternoon Express by John-Paul Cleary

A tangle of wires and tubes were going in and out of him. Some led to the mobile care pack strapped to his chest while others such as his oxygen tube and urinary catheter were connected directly to the service ports in the seat itself. He didn't open his eyes when I got on the train, pushing my heavy bag under the seat, but I could tell from the rhythmic beat of his ventilator he was still alive. The sound of the machine and the electronic buzz of his other equipment joined with the collective drone of personal health systems and the train's own appliances in action throughout the carriage. I looked around. I was in the minority on this train. Almost every other seat was taken by a white or hairless head, each bobbing and moving on loose necks in time with the motion of the train.

I slid into the seat opposite. I wouldn't normally be on the train this early in the afternoon but this wasn't a normal day. I checked my watch and tried to relax but my heart was pumping with excitement. Just a few more minutes and this journey would be over for the very last time. It was both an ending and a beginning.

The old man grunted in his sleep. He and others like him were the reason I had ended up here. He was an extreme geriatric, part of a generation who had simply refused to die. Following up behind them was another generation who were doing the same, then another and another. Their stubborn reluctance to throw off this mortal coil had created a social traffic jam from which there was no escape. They held onto the best jobs, the best properties and had all the money. There was nothing anyone could do about it. As a social group they were so large and so powerful they dictated most political decisions. This led to an ever tightening circle of concessions to themselves and increased investment into geriatric care to keep them alive for even longer.

Really they should already be dead.

My generation found ourselves growing up in a world where everything was already taken. There was no longer any notion of wealth passing from one generation to another. The natural order of things had stalled. I thought about how hard I worked but still my wife and children were squashed into that tiny chance-house. Like many other families we'd had to throw ourselves on the mercy of the government. At least it meant we had a roof over our heads.

I looked at the old man and his wrinkled immobile face, his sparse wispy grey hair. This was his fault. Why wouldn't he just die? I wanted them all to die.

I tapped the table dividing us and the electronic display loomed into focus under the table-top. It was a terrible design. To look at it you had to bend your head at a ninety degree angle leaving you with a stiff neck after about a minute. Also the outer surface was so scratched and scuffed it was like reading though a net curtain. It was solid though, well-made and would probably last forever.

I wanted something quick and superficial so I chose the front page news. There had been four more successful attacks in the last few days: 2000 geriatric holidaymakers killed when their superjumbo blew up; 600 when a spa had been destroyed by an incendiary device; and another 1500 when two trains derailed, both mid-day 'geriatric expresses' like this one. That meant over 4000 fewer geriatrics in the world. It was a drop in the ocean but it was a start. Thousands of houses and jobs freed up for the rest of us. Now at least some could start living the lives of which the older generations had deprived us. And there would be more to follow.

The old man still hadn't opened his eyes. I wondered where he found to go during the day. Where did any of them find to go? It was amazing he could still get around on his own. How old was he? 145? 150? There was a Japanese woman in the news who was 197, only three years from the landmark 200. It was only a matter of time. Where would it end? The planet was already bulging at the seams.

The explosive device didn't make a sound, not to my ears.

One moment I was staring over at the old man then time was suspended and everything took flight. There was an incredible feeling of weightlessness, of taking off, of flying.

Then I started rolling. I fell from my seat and was thrown around like a ball. I smashed my head off something solid and kept turning over and over. I was aware of things bashing hard into me. Random objects, cases, bags, portable computers and people. We were all rolling together, jarring each other, falling on each other, hurting each other. We were unable to stop. Everything flew past me so quickly I couldn't focus. I was forever moving, forever falling but there was no ground there to meet me.

My body started pumping hormones, overriding the negative physical sensations. I reached a sensory and emotional nirvana and the pain drifted away.

When everything came to rest I was lying in a pile of luggage on the ceiling which was now the floor. The carriage was upside-down. Pains were shooting throughout my body. I couldn't tell where one pain ended and another began. How seriously was I injured? I stretched out one of my arms which seemed to respond. I could feel both my legs. There was a strong salty coppery taste in my mouth. I touched my head and my fingers came back dipped in blood. Now I'd found a head injury it started to hurt. I realised it was serious but at least I was alive.

Across the carriage people were moaning and shouting. I pushed obstructions away and sat up. Pain rattled up my spine. Something large loomed above me, swinging slowly back and forth. It was the old man. He was awake now. Somehow during the crash he had become entangled in his own equipment, primarily the oxygen tube which had wrapped itself around his neck and was slowly strangling him. His knees, trapped under the table, were all that stopped the oxygen tube from snuffing out his life. But it wouldn't be long. I could see it tightening around his neck. He saw me. His eyes widened, silently pleading for my aid.

I thought about my family in the cramped little chance-house and about all our struggles and the hopelessness I felt every morning I woke. This man dangling above me was the cause of it all. He and his generation were strangling the life out of our world just as the tube was strangling the life out of him. It would be a fitting end. It would be a fitting end for all of them. For a moment I didn't move.

But today I had solved my problems. I'd signed us up for off-world exploration and colonisation and the approval came through at lunchtime. I'd resigned my job on the spot which was why I was taking the afternoon train home. Going off-world would be dangerous but it couldn't be any worse than what we'd leave behind. I struggled to my feet nodding to the old man. I couldn't let him die no matter how unfair the world was. I was no terrorist.

I climbed onto the upturned table, reached up and started helping him down to safety.

About the author: John-Paul Cleary lives in the small town of Stonehaven in the North East of Scotland. His debut novel Convergent Space peaked at number 1 in the Space Opera charts on Amazon UK in 2012 and has consistently featured in the top five for more than six months.

John Paul's blog is here; convergentspace.blog.co.uk

The Removal Man by David K. Paterson

Ah, there you are. Malcolm asked me to stop by and tell you that he'll be a bit late. Do you mind if I sit? These old joints can't take standing up for too long. I hope you'll join me in a quick drink while we wait. We ought to commemorate the fortieth anniversary of the Allied victory over the Nazis, after all. Oh, but you think that was in 1945, don't you? Well, you'd be surprised at just how much history didn't actually happen. The only reason you think it did is because of my colleagues and I. We're the Removal Men.

No, you haven't heard of us. Just like you haven't heard of Sergei Antonov, the man who held the Soviet Union in an iron grip after Lenin. Stalin, you say? Well, I'm impressed. You know your history or, rather, our version of history. The one where Antonov never existed, as far as anyone knows. Stalin still had to take the blame for Antonov's tamer excesses, though. You can only do so much, especially when it affects that many people. Someone dies, we can't bring them back. We just make sure that the reasons they died are more... palatable than the truth.

So, you can imagine that Nazi Germany was a huge amount of work for us, after four decades. The world doesn't remember Klaus Adelmann, Inge Speck and the others who came after Hitler. If you think that the horrors he wrought achieved a whole new level of evil, think yourself lucky you don't have my memories. Of course, when the atrocities are truly awful enough, the truth we've tried to remove can seep through into the collective consciousness, despite our best efforts. You've heard of the film, "Soylent Green"? That's just the tip of the iceberg. I think you can see why the world needs to remember Korea, Vietnam and countless Cold War conflicts instead. We provide a history that people can cope with. One that lets them feel hope and respect towards others, rather than fear and hate. And, touch wood, we haven't had to remove a global memory since that June day in 1972. Perhaps this time. Perhaps.

It's not just major events like wars. We're busy all the time. Did you know that nine hundred thousand people disappear every year? They say goodbye to their families and go to the shop or go to work or start their drive home and, just like that, they're gone. Parents, husbands, wives, waiting at home, holding on to the hope that one day, they'll come back. That's our rule. Remember the victims, forget the villains. People are always doing terrible things to each other. Things that no one should have to remember. Things no one does, thanks to us. It's much better to have the possibility of a happy ending than to have knowledge of the absolute opposite, sometimes.

Speaking of which, did you know our first ever removal was Doctor James Deacon? Sorry, I'm being stupid. Of course you don't. Certainly, it wasn't our finest hour and it wasn't a great job, but it was 1888 and, to be fair, no one today links that name to Jack the Ripper. Nor do they remember the autumn that the streets of Whitechapel ran red with blood, so it all worked out in the end. That removal took three weeks, with Mister Babbage's Difference Engine Number Three running nonstop. Remarkable machine and a remarkable man. It's a shame we had to remove it, but when the Austro-Hungarian Empire got hold of the plans, it put the world onto a fast track to tragedy. Mister Babbage understood what had to be done. Ironically, he was the first person to see the potential of removing undesirable memories. Of course, things were simpler then, back in the day. With only the telephone and telegraph to send news, it was easy to remove what needed to be removed before too many people found out. The last few years have really taken it out of us, though. Dozens of websites storing every last bit of news the second it happens, with seven billion people a click away. I swear, we put more computing power into editing the Web than we do editing people.

Oh, it's really amusingly simple to change memories. People's minds are quite susceptible to alteration. After all, the brain's just an organic computer. Send out a strong enough signal and you can make the world forget. We just press the little red button on this device. Here, let me demonstrate. Oh, don't worry. Just some insignificant memories, slipping from people's minds like the grains of sand in an hourglass.

Well, I've finished my drink. Thank you for listening to an old man's stories. I have to tell you, if I didn't have the chances to get these things off my chest, I don't think I could keep doing this job. Knowing one version of history, but having to pretend that another is real? It does take it out of you and, of course, the job isn't really compatible with personal relationships. The acute awareness that, if you miss just one tiny detail, something that might seem insignificant to you, it could let the truth slip out. It might be to one person, but then that person talks or texts or tweets and then, like a failing dam, the truth would begin to leak out, the stream becoming stronger and stronger, and we know how that would end, don't we? A rushing flood of raw, unadulterated, sickening truth, crashing over humanity and carrying away their precious, palatable world, leaving total destruction in its path.

Goodness, I have become quite melodramatic in my old age, haven't I? Anyway, I'm sure you realise that no one can know about any of this, but then, that's not going to be a problem as far as you're concerned. Not at all.

You don't remember how you got here, do you? You don't know where you're going. And if I'm not mistaken, by now you barely remember your own name, let alone anyone else's. Fear not, I will remember it for the rest of my days. I will hold the memories of what you and Malcolm did to all those people, so believe me when I tell you this will be a relief.

Oh, don't make a fuss. It won't help. It was your choice to do the things you did. You can blame your parents, your Dark Passenger or the voices in your head, but in the end, you chose to do those things. I know you don't remember any of them, but your choices led you to this moment and now you have to face the consequences. I wish I could walk away, I really do. I wish I could leave you to carry on in blissful ignorance, but we can only change memories and I know that the thing that drives you to do what you do is buried somewhere deeper than that. Call it bad chemistry or call it a tainted soul, it doesn't make any difference to us. We know you'll do those things again eventually.

We've seen it time and time again.

It's human nature. It's what keeps us so busy.

About the author: This is the second story by David K. Paterson in this anthology.

Cat's Eye by Peter Holz

'It's dead, Jim.'

Jim nudged the motionless cat with the toe of his boot and peered at its unmoving form. 'Are you sure?' He thought he caught a flicker of movement and bent down for a closer look. Its eye. Something about its eye. There was movement there. Could it be? There was someone in there. Tiny hands pressed against the inside of the cat's cornea. An anguished and contorted mouth silently formed the words, 'I can't get out'.

Jim recoiled in shock and struggled to his feet, face pale. 'I guess you're right,' he murmured uncertainly to his companion.

'Come on, or we'll be late for the movie'.

Jim followed his friend, the image of the prisoner voicing his silent scream burnt into his head. Try as he might he could not get the picture out of his skull. Not even the steamy sex scene distracted him from the plight of the little fellow. After the movie he excused himself from the usual post-film drinking session and wandered back to find the cat.

The feline's prostrate form was as he last saw it, unmoving before the heavy wooden door. He approached it cautiously, heart pounding with each step. Pausing over the body Jim knelt down slowly to gaze once more into its unseeing eye.

The figure was still there, position unchanged from before, still mouthing his silent plea. Jim stared at him intently and shrugged his shoulders as if to say, 'What can I do?'

The tiny figure began gesticulating wildly, pounding his diminutive fists against the cat's cornea, trying to break through. Finally he collapsed in exhaustion, head resting against the inside of the cat's eye.

Steeling his resolve, Jim reached into his pocket and pulled out a pen knife. Carefully, he opened up the blade and dragged the dead cat closer. The small figure looked up, backed away into the corner of the eye, and pointed at the cat's cornea, finger jabbing repeatedly at the spot where Jim should make his cut.

Slowly, deliberately Jim punctured the cornea with his knife. A clear viscous jelly popped out onto the cat's face, the small figure flowing with it. At first the figure lay unmoving on the cat's cheek but then it began to grow, expanding until the cat's body had disappeared beneath the bulk of a fully grown man.

Wet from being bathed in the cat's ocular fluids the man got to his feet and looked at Jim. 'Am I ever glad you came along. You have no idea how long I've been stuck in there.'

Jim stared and gulped. 'But how did you get in there?'

The other man smiled. 'Do you believe in the hereafter? Well I never did. I had myself a pretty good life going in the here and now, but I always hated cats'. He looked disdainfully at the body of the cat with the punctured eye. 'They skulk around; kill little birds just for the fun of it. It used to make me sick. So, I put bait out and shot the slimy bastards. There was this one particular tom, real big bugger he was. I got him a beauty in the side of the head.

'Then one day I found myself crossing the road on the wrong side of a bus. A brief moment of excruciating pain, followed by total darkness and the next thing I know I'm seeing the world from inside a cat. Reincarnation. My penance for shooting the buggers. Horrible though, licking your own balls, eating dead birds. Fortunately we were cleaned up by a milk truck and I was free again. At least I should have been. But my soul failed to eject. I worked my way round to its eye, window to the soul and all that. And that's when you found me and set me free. I can't tell you how grateful I am.

The only trouble is, now I'm a soul without a body. Anything happens to me and I'm gone for all eternity. Say, you look familiar. Do I know you?'

The man looked intently at Jim, whose lips had curled back in a grin to reveal prominent canines. Jim turned sideways so an old wound, such as might have been caused by a gunshot, was visible on the side of his head.

Before the man could draw another breath, retractable claws had emerged and slashed. He collapsed to the ground, blood gushing from lacerations in his neck. Jim smiled as the man's consciousness dimmed and went out. As he walked away the lifeless body turned to vapour and dissipated on the breeze, carrying with it the faint sound of purring.

About the author: Peter Holz graduated from veterinary school in 1987. He spent the following 25 years trying to turn himself into a zoo/wildlife veterinarian, while travelling the world, getting married and having two kids, only to realize that he was in fact a frustrated writer and not a veterinarian at all.

Night Watch by Apeksha Harsh

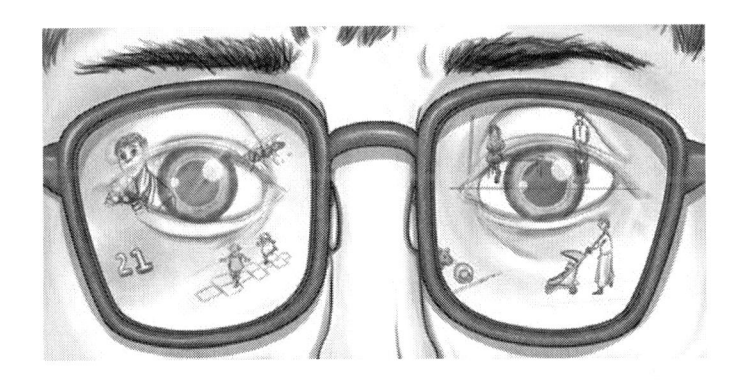

'Your eyes are getting worse, Mr Neat.' The doctor handed a pair of spectacles to the man sitting across from him.

Mr Neat smiled a thin, long smile.

'You know, lenses are so much better,' continued the doctor.

'It gives me a terrible itch,' Mr Neat said in a slow, hoarse voice. He unfolded the new spectacles, fixed them over his face and blinked.

'We only use the best, Mr Neat. And you wouldn't have to see me all the time.'

Mr Neat tilted his neck from one side to the other, each time cracking his knuckles against his neck. He stared with his bug-like eyes at the doctor. 'Would you like me to poke you in the eye, Doctor?'

The ophthalmologist squirmed a little in his seat.

Mr Neat's lips stretched out into a widening smile and his teeth shone under the yellow clinic light.

'Just as I thought, you don't like things in your eyes, either.'

Mr Neat slipped his hands inside his coat pockets. 'Good day, Doctor,' he said as he walked out the door.

Outside, he looked up into the sky at the orange ball of a sun. His eyes focused and refocused on the blinding light. 'Much better,' he said.

He crossed the pavement and passed kids playing in the street. Some of them, it seemed, still knew what hopscotch was. They jumped over chalk boxes they had crudely drawn on the stone. Mr Neat could see the chalk lines were broken and uneven. He could see there were little pockmarks in the grey stone. He could even see a tiny black ant scurrying to avoid pink buckled shoes. Children. They could be so violent.

Just three more minutes of brisk walking and he would be home. Mr Neat's gaze swept the street – quickly and then with more precision. A girl in a red skirt read Dostoevsky at a bus stop. A boy with five holes in his left shoe stared at her. At the corner of the street, a mother was waiting with her baby in a pram. Its heavily chewed pacifier had fallen onto the ground and a slick black rat was scampering towards it.

Mr Neat stopped watching and he stopped walking. He was outside a blue door with the number '21' on it. A blue door in line with five other blue doors. He had reached his house.

Once inside, Mr Neat removed a salad he had prepared from his refrigerator. The ice lettuce was a few days old and the plum tomatoes were reddeningly ripe. This would be enough to leave him a little hungry.

He ate quietly, standing in the kitchen and watched as a few shreds of salad fell to the floor. When he was done eating, he went into his room. The clock on the side-table said that it was two hours to bedtime. Mr Neat changed into pyjamas that had yellow stars on them. 'Twinkle, twinkle,' he said in a sing-song voice as he got under the covers and looked at the window.

Mr Neat sat in his bed with the covers tucked round his legs. He swayed his head from side to side, from side to side. 'Twinkle, twinkle,' he said in a raspy voice.

For the next two hours, Mr Neat waited and swayed his head. Then he took off his spectacles and stared at the wall in front of him. It was a bit blurry but he could make out the crack at the top where the spider was hiding. Spectacles were far better than contact lenses. And his vision wasn't too bad for a forty-two year old.

The sun had gone down and night was taking over. In a few minutes, all that Mr Neat would see would be a fierce black sky and a piece of moon. He shook his shoulders to relax them and waited. His room grew dark and a shaft of pale moonlight dropped down through the window. Mr Neat smiled. It was time for bed.

He stretched his arms into the air and then wiped his hands over his face. He traced a circle over each eye. 'Twinkle, twinkle,' he said with a grin. He dug his fingers into his eye sockets and tugged at his eyeballs. The slime seeped under his nails and his eyes turned and twisted like they were spinning inside a washing machine. Then in one clean motion, Mr Neat pulled out his eyeballs. They made a large 'pop' sound.

The eyes in his hands looked at his empty bloodless sockets. The eyelids blinked and Mr Neat yawned. He placed his eyes on the side-table. The optic nerves left clear drops on the wood. They were not covered in blood and they ended in perfect little bows.

Mr Neat lay down in bed. In a minute, he was fast asleep.

The eyes trembled in their thin tear films as the moonlight hit them. The pupils dilated and Mr Neat mumbled in his sleep.

The moon warmed the eyeballs, making them glow with a lunar shine. Their vision was not blurred anymore. Their vision was far better than it could ever have been with the new spectacles. They could perceive dust-mites crawling in the darkness and the twitching of the trapped fly as the spider in the crack broke off its wings and then two of its legs.

Mr Neat's eyes were watching his house.

As the night continued, one of the eyeballs rolled off the table. Like a tiny golden globe it sped across the carpet. It stopped at the entrance to the kitchen and shook off the stray hairs and grungy carpet fibers. Something slick and black was gnawing at the floor. It lifted its head, the skin of a red tomato hanging from its pointy teeth. Its stomach bulged oddly. The eyeball rocked back and forth and then raced back through the house to the room where Mr Neat was asleep. Slick and black followed immediately.

The eyeball rolled with ease onto the corner of the sheet hanging over the bed. It travelled across the mattress and glowed brightly. Then it waited. Nimble feet dashed across the room, leaped onto the sheet and scurried towards the shiny eyeball. As the black rodent rushed onto the bed with teeth bared, a hand pressed around its body. Mr Neat brought the rat up to his face. The gleaming eyeball was rocking round in one socket.

'Hello, hello,' said Mr Neat dipping a finger into his other empty eye cavity. 'It's a good thing that salad left me a bit hungry.'

The rat squirmed but Mr Neat only clamped his grip harder. 'Don't be like that... everyone has to eat.' He grinned. 'Besides, I've been waiting.'

The rat squealed and frantically wiggled its feet. 'Don't worry. I won't break your legs off like our spider friend,' said Mr Neat at his raspy best.

He tightened his fist around the rat's stomach. Its eyes bulged and Mr Neat gave it a tremendous squeeze. A pacifier coated in bile and blood popped out onto his bed. Mr Neat laughed a little as the rat shivered in his hand. As he squeezed harder, he felt its heartbeat weaken and die away.

Mr Neat then put his warm meal into his mouth and slowly crunched. He did not have any trouble with the bones or the coarse hairs. He brushed the pacifier off the bed and then stuck his fingers into his eye hole. He pulled out the eyeball one more time and placed it on the table to soak in the moonlight, right next to the other eye.

'A pity the moon only comes out at night,' said Mr Neat, the hollows in his face turned towards the window. 'Reduced to wearing spectacles.'

He stretched his arms into the air and then wiped his hands over his face. There was so much to keep watch for each night. Sometimes, his glowing eyeballs would even watch from the steps outside the blue door that read '21'. Things were always more fascinating under the moonlight.

Mr Neat curled his toes as he wrapped the covers round himself. Time for bed.

'Twinkle, twinkle,' he mumbled happily as he went back to sleep.

About the author: Apeksha is a keen poet and a fledgling storyteller who studied the MA in Writing at Warwick. She enjoys imparting the joys of writing to others (preferably those who come of their own free will). She likes dancing and occasionally talks in strange accents that perhaps only she understands.

The Monkey's Kiss by Brad Greenwood

JULY 27, 2034
SPACE TRAVEL SPECIAL
TIME
Errol 'Dickey' Dickinson

Something bothers me every time I look at that damned picture. Those puckered, simian lips blowing hot, stinky air into Dickey's face. Dickey's smile spanned ear to ear, his eye closest to the monkey squinting and nose wrinkling as though being pecked by a sweet old lady who had just eaten canned tuna; adorable and revolting at the same time.

I often wonder how many business men, school kids and stay-at-home mums had the same reaction when they glimpsed the silver image on newsstands and coffee tables around the world.

My great grandpa's original black and white, ten by eight was now hanging on my studio wall; the same photograph that had graced the cover of Time Magazine a hundred years earlier. The iconic portrait launched his career as a photo journalist and made Dickinson Aerospace a household name.

The horn sounded, the driver was getting impatient. I packed my Nikon and spoke quietly to the ghost of my great grandpa. I wasn't really interested in speaking to God; I preferred the idea of praying to someone who I knew existed at some point in time.

The driver was chatty. 'Christ, your great granddaddy took that picture huh? Sorry, bud, but it gives me the creeps.'

I didn't say anything but this jerk had a point. The Monkey's Kiss lacked genuine affection. The gesture, despite its comical nature, was cynical and mechanical, a simple instruction from a trainer to kiss the brainy human. It was all for show. The image was a symbol of man's conquest over the lesser species. I couldn't help but feel they hated us for it. We were now ready to conquer the universe, but first we would have to enlist the non-consensual assistance of a monkey.

A gigantic beauty lounging in her underwear floated over the western distributor. She seemed to be watching the sky as well. The driver took his eyes off the road and pointed to the billboard. 'Hey bud, you ever shoot any of those hot models?'

I still get nervous before a big assignment. Photo journalism is about moments. Not just capturing moments but anticipating them. You've got to say to yourself *here it comes* and just shoot and *bam*, there it is.

The driver turned onto the motorway, still yapping. 'Bet you've shagged a few of those models too, hey, bud?'

I wanted this idiot to shut up. 'Sure, bud.' I said.

As we crossed the bridge I could see the pontoon in the distance and beyond that the big, beautiful sky. I sat forward and pushed my face into the windscreen looking for the glowing white hot star that would signal re-entry.

I'd never met Dickey before. This would be the first time and possibly the last; Jesus, the guy is 150 years old, literally. But if today proved successful and that damn monkey pops its head out of the hatch not more than a week older, then who knows, maybe Dickey will have begun the journey to immortality.

Errol 'Dickey' Dickinson is a man of extraordinary wealth and ambition. When Richard Branson (still on ice waiting for a new pancreas to grow) was sending civilians to the moon Dickey had his sights set on broader horizons. He had hoped to be the first to eclipse the boundaries of space and time itself.

Although no one has seen a macaque monkey for 30 years, they've been pretty much wiped out, there was a time when they were abundant and performed regularly for a captive human audience in a sort of primate vaudeville. It was in one such gig Dickey watched fascinated as a monkey sat at a table with a sling shot and a bowl of fruit. It fired the fruit into the heavens like David trying to slay an invisible Goliath. Then it tied a napkin around its hairy neck and held up a big aluminium fork until each piece of fruit landed neatly, one at a time, impaled on the prongs. There was a round of applause then riotous laughter as Dickey was clocked in the forehead with a flying lychee. Everyone looked up to see a second monkey perched high in a tree. It caught the fruit launched from the sling shot and dropped it on cue.

So when Dickey built his own sling shot; five hundred thousand metric tons of metal and fuel perched on a steel scaffold sixty stories high like some kind of monolithic Mechano toy; what better pilot to travel at the speed of light than a grinning macaque.

To this day Dickey's proprietary propulsion system is as closely guarded a secret as the Colonel's eleven herbs and spices. Although it didn't achieve the speed predicted it is believed to have managed a pace regarded as a triumph in Einsteinian physics.

The theory is at such a speed time itself slows down… one hundred years of earth time is a single week inside the nine hundred billion dollar tin can. This monkey would be the first living being to travel into the future. The question of course is what could we expect when the can gets kicked back into our orbit 100 years since its launch?

I made my way to the front of the press tent as the first wave rocked the pontoon. You couldn't hear anything beyond the chatter of excited media and the flapping of the marquee canvas. An official reached out and gripped my shoulder. 'We have splash down… let's move.'

I held tightly to the guard rail with one hand and protected my camera with the other as the retrieval vessel bounced over the rippling ocean. Through the mist of sea spray I could see the sun reflecting off a metallic object bobbing in the surf. I was almost afraid to look at him. It was a face I had seen so often, but now I was seeing at him in the flesh. Dickey's skin was tanned and smooth, his silver hair thick and healthy. His eyes sparkled more than the ocean. It was remarkable; the man really didn't seem to be a day over 60. He smiled at me and said loudly, 'Today is a great day, young man!'

I kind of raised my camera and nodded, then he added, 'Don't leave the lens cap on. The world won't want to miss this.'

The airlock hissed and cracked open. I viewed the world now only through my lens. The glass became foggy; I wiped it and when I refocused a grinning, wide-eyed primate was staring down the barrel. A couple of guys wrestled the creature as it flayed about baring its teeth and flaring its nostrils. The damn monkey had done it, travelling faster than ever thought possible and defying the known limits of time and space. Maybe that's why its eyes looked horribly bloodshot. Dickey grappled with it, like a parent trying to settle a naughty child. 'Come on give us a kiss!' he spat. My great grandpa's ghost urged me to seize the moment. I pressed the shutter button.

The Pulitzer Prize was not for the monkey tearing Dickey's ear off, but for what came a moment before; something chilling; something I saw coming. Maybe my great grandpa did too. In many respects maybe the world did. The monkey leaned in to the side of Dickey's head, cupped its child-like hand around Dickey's ear as though whispering to him. From the dying smile on Dickeys face and the terror in his eyes perhaps it actually did.

About the author: As a child Brad Greenwood had no doubt that ghosts and UFOs were real. Now in his 40s, Brad continues to indulge his fascination in the mysteries of the universe through film making, art and fiction. He lives in Sydney, Australia.

The Warrior Woman by Joanna Vandenbring

'Don't move!' sounded his hoarse cry. Oh, she could tell that his Barbarian throat was as dry as hers after the long dance of iron and blood down the slopes and crags of Glen Uswar until they reached the shallow mountain stream that led straight to the holy well.

'Can you hear me? Do not move!'

All at once she was focussed again. She was standing in the midst of the stream, ankle deep in water and the pale foreigner with the pink nose was moving slowly, gracefully, towards her and in his hands were a sword and a mallet. Legend had it that he had received those arms from the mountain trolls. Naturally it was all nonsense. She had chipped that blade and she had bloody chipped him too. In a sudden burst of confidence she gathered her forces and smiled defiantly as she leapt backwards, out of the water and onto the boulders behind.

'Go home to the abomination that spawned you, you little milk-suckler!'

There was nobody who could climb an almost flat rock surface like her, even single handed she was still faster and more able than warriors half her age. Whichever way he turned she would follow him from above and set in for the kill as he tried to approach one of the three exits from the gully. He seemed horrified by her climb.

'For the sake of the gods, get down from there! You will bleed to death!'

Her laughter echoed between the narrow walls of the ravine. Far away the wolves howled, as if in answer. Then it was all silent again, except for the gurgling of the water and the sound of her heart in her ears. What was he doing? It was so dark. She had to fight to keep her balance with that damned right arm hanging limp and soaked in warm liquid. Now she could hear him clanking with his sword.

'Listen, soldier. I am coming up for you!'

Sword on his back, he was climbing the rock face not much slower than her. She could smell his fear on the night breeze and she could hear him breathe faster and faster but he was climbing and she was faltering. Somehow her brain must have taken a serious blow too, because she was finding it hard to visualise her next step.

Then an iron clamp closed around her ankle.

'Let go of me!' She kicked herself free from his grip but that made the two of them lose their balance. For a moment it seemed as if they would both fall headlong onto the boulders. Then she regained her balance and he heaved himself up, gaining full control of her battered body. She could feel his strained breaths.

'Now you shall have to come down with me! Enough now!'

Before she could work out how best to fling them both down onto the boulders, he somehow managed to haul the two of them halfway down and by the time she had found strength for a risky backwards blow there was only a short distance to fall.

He landed on his feet and immediately reached for his sword. She grabbed for it, too, bringing him down, slipping and sliding.

They tumbled down the last bit, a mass of legs, arms, fists and hard knees, and for a few moments she had no clue what was him and what was her. She had suddenly visualised the movements needed to retrieve her own precious sword, but when she tried to rise, her adversary shot after and flung her up the uneven rock wall as if she had been a rag doll.

'It is time to give in now! You give in and I shall…'

She spat a curse at him that would probably guarantee her a place in the darkest and coldest corner of the Fields of Despair and then she spat some saliva too and she could see the naked rage in those pale eyes just below hers.

Then she was down.

Struggling to register what had happened she first thought that he had broken her neck the way she had read in his eyes that he wished to. But her neck was neither broken nor slit. Her feet were clammy and wet inside the fine reindeer moccasins and she thought with shame that she must have wet herself, then she remembered that she had stepped in the waters of the little mountain stream that led all the way to the sacred well. Oh, how she had angered the goddesses today.

'You are not going to move again. Do you hear me, yes or no? You are also not going to spit at me again for then I shall have to knock you out for a longer while!'

That odious man who stunk of cow milk had simply knocked her out. That was what had happened. Oh, great goddess of mercy and war, was he going to make a slow process of it?

She looked at the stars and the moon and the eternal skies and wondered if that was where she would be going now. It was night and they had been fighting almost all day and now she would pass on to another set of stars and moon and skies. What if they weren't as pretty as these ones?

'Yield!' wheezed the man, standing there victorious with one foot heavy on her chest, sword raised above his head. The clean upper parts of its blade glimmered in the faint moonlight.

'Bastard!' coughed she from between clenched teeth. A warrior of her rank had spent years of training for a situation like this and she had only reached her position because she learned her lessons well.

'Yield, I said.'

She didn't reply. The full moon was shining in full splendour and she hoped that he could see the hatred in her eyes. His eyes were pale, but not as pale as those of many of his people, somewhere in between hazel and gold, and there was compassion rather than dislike in them.

'You do want to live, I assume?'

'I could not care less.'

He sighed and sheathed his stained sword, wrenching her unwounded right arm backwards and upwards in an iron grip. Without a word he searched her, coolly and mechanically, and extricated the little dagger that she, like all her fellow sisters, kept inserted in the swaddles with which they kept their bosoms in place. She waited for him to rape her. It was what a warrior did who wanted to humiliate but not kill his enemy, but this one was apparently a dispassionate professional. He wasn't tall, but damn it if he wasn't about the strongest man she had encountered.

As he leaned over her he wrung her arm a further half inch upwards and she envisioned herself abandoned at the bottom a ravine with one arm half cut off and the other with the bones jutting out. Then she felt a calloused hand with tight wrappings around it that pulled the hair away from her face and an unshaven, sweaty cheek pressed closed to hers.

'Listen, soldier, you have the time until I have counted to ten to tell me that you yield.'

He spoke with a foreign accent, but far from unintelligible like some of his people. She closed her eyes and inside her mind she said a prayer to the goddess of war and revenge. He was counting and she was keeping her eyes closed so that his sweat wouldn't drip into her eyes.

Then she was free. Blood rushed back to her arm and she almost cried out in pain as it did so but only almost.

'You're well trained, soldier.' said that odd voice.

She licked her dry lips and to her surprise, she felt the taste of someone else's blood. It hadn't been sweat that he leaked on her. She glanced over her shoulder in his direction and saw that blood was oozing down the side of his not entirely unpleasant Barbarian face.

'Do not mock me.'

'I am not mocking you. You are damned good.'

'Give me back my sword!' She was crouching on the ground, trying to rub her left hand with the right but her body was not working as it should. Her ears were ringing, her right arm senseless and her back refused to straighten. Eternal curses on the Old Mother who had sent her after him alone!

'Listen soldier, you will never see that sword again. It is mine now.' He gave her precious sword a contemptuous kick so that it ended far beyond her reach, just by the undernourished little birch trees that lined the sides of the ravine where their long fight had ended. It was his by right. As was she.

'What are you going to do with me?'

'With you?' he frowned questioningly as he extracted something from one of the pockets of his fringed leather leggings.

'Yes?'

'If you have decided that you wish to live then I will try to stitch up that gash in your arm and maybe steady the bones with some splints, that is what I will do with you.' said he and pressed a wad of wool against his wounded ear.

He patched them both up right there in the middle of the wilderness and she was surprised at his healing skills. She had never ever suspected that a useless clod-eater could be so deft at suturing a gash and even less that he would have a pouch of healing herbs with him ready for use, so when he had finished she decided to relent.

'Thank you, Chief Keifas.' said she grudgingly.

'So you know who I am? '

'Of course I do.'

'I did not think a woman would have dared fight me if she had known who I was.'

'Whyever not?'

Then he smiled and she told herself not to let his disarming smile and glittering mane impress her. The Old Woman had warned her of that.

'I am not going to mention the fact that as lord of all the lands between the southern seas and the eternal ice I would be entitled to condemn not only you but your whole family to forfeiture of their right to own, live and possess for…'

'Yes?'

'Yes. And besides…you are but a *woman*.'

'I am a sister of the sacred allegiance community.'

'I guessed as much.' He stared haughtily at her through the moonshine and all of a sudden it was as if the light brown in his eyes melted to gold and he let a light twitch play with the corners of his mouth, but he didn't smile. Instead he bowed and brought his hands tight together on his chest in a gesture of reverence.

She stared at him and wondered what to do. He made part of a universe that she had spent a lifetime combating, spiritually and physically. The chieftain's people were stationary: accepting the customs of the peoples from the south they had decided to start growing crops and to stay put in highly fortified enclaves. The territories that they claimed were vast and those who had chosen not to settle down had to pull further and further northwards in direction of the mountains and the plains and the eternal ice.

They both sat down on a large boulder and drank some sort of invigorating liquid from a flask that he had brought.

She noticed that he was watching her with curiosity and something like fear.

'You were contracted to kill me, weren't you?'

'No. I was ordered to do so.'

'Will you be expelled from the order now?'

'No. But they might send me off to meditate in some very remote location.'

'Come with me, and I shall find a decent hard-working husband for you.'

She winced and fought hard to stay serious, but in the end she doubled up laughing instead.

'I am perfectly serious.'

'Chieftain, I have been called by the gods to serve them in this way. It is not a matter of choice.'

'Do you seriously think that the gods call people to assassinate others?'

She looked the other way and shivered in a chilly night breeze that she hadn't noticed before.

'What is your name, soldier?'

'Deenah.'

'I am honoured to meet you. I have never actually talked to one of the sacred sisters before.'

'I shall fight you again if you let me go.'

'I know.'

They sat there for a while, side by side in the silent night. Then he started speaking again.

'Come home with me. You would have a good life with my people, a safe life…'

'My lord, I have lived more than forty summers. I am past the age when women get married.'

'Forty? Well, I say…' he raised an eyebrow and smiled, 'I have plenty of retainers of a certain age who are widowers who would find someone like you quite a good match.'

'You are not in jest at all, are you?'

'Far from it.'

They looked at each other and she thought again how odd it was that a great chieftain like him should be so short. But then he was nothing like the unnameable enemy she had imagined him to be.

'Chieftain, you said I was free to go.'

'You are.'

'Then I shall have to go now.' She rose and bit her teeth together in order to block out the dull pain that was making itself ever more present. 'Good bye, may the goddesses walk with you always, chieftain.'

'Thank you for your good wishes, Deenah of the Sacred Allegiance.' He had been busy trying to bandage his swollen and black ankle, but now he looked at her through the shadows again. 'But why don't you camp here tonight? I shall strike a fire to keep the wolves away and if I can find my provisioning pouch, then I will also cook some food.'

She looked up at the stars high above the sacred path. The wolves had indeed taken up their wild song in the distance, but she wasn't afraid. Her mind was busy analysing the lessons that the gods had sent her way today and that made her smile although her body was aching. There are ends and there are beginnings and for her this was a new beginning. She knew that but she did not understand which road the goddesses wanted that beginning to take.

'I shall not lie with you, chieftain.' said she after a long inner deliberation.

'Did I ask you to, priestess?'

'But I might share a fire with you, if you would agree to that.'

Then he laughed and tried standing on his swollen leg.

'Excellent! Then you might ponder upon my suggestion over night. I can assure you that there are fine men among my retainers that you might want to share more than a fire with...'

'Chieftain, I have told you that mine is a calling!'

She watched him closely from the corner of her eye and she could tell he was trying to wheedle her into making a choice that would suit his scopes. Whatever they were.

'Oh. Yes. I almost forgot.'

Deenah sat there and watched him as he lit the camp fire and cooked a rather mysterious stew that he claimed contained dried meat but possibly had bits of bark in it, and as she relaxed and forgot to fear him, she realised that she would have to let the goddess of war and revenge decide for her in her dreams. It was not for her to make a choice.

About the author: Joanna Vandenbring is forty-two years old and an EFL teacher in Italy where she has lived since she was twenty-one, although she teaches in the UK during the summer holidays. In the 1980s and 1990s some of her short stories and poems were published in various European magazines. She has a PhD in History and has written articles on guerrilla warfare. In her free time she walks with her dogs, reads books and listens to music.

The Star Worker by Sarah Cuming

Today was Yule. She had no calendar to tell her, no dates etched out in stone, but she knew it as a certainty. Months spent staring at the shadows cast by sandstone sundials hadn't taught her, it was something she could feel on a marrow-deep level. Cassie had always loved the open spaces as a child, adored the contrasts between hot and cold and watched the colour changes of the trees with rapture. Then her magic had come, found that part of her soul that defined what she was, and multiplied everything tenfold. The cold could no longer bite so hard, but became a secondary part of her, assaulting her senses such that she knew precisely how it worked. She could use it.

And so she had taken her magic and became a Star Worker, a point of light against the darkness that threatened everything. Against the Void.

She was using it now, her Nature Magic, moulding and turning it back on itself until cold became warmth, keeping her internal organs alive in this killer landscape. She had been thrown here by one of the Void Workers.

She had been fighting with him, assaulting with flame and root and cracking earth in her attempts to push him back from where he had been massacring the town's council. He worked with weight, lifting boulders and trees and bits of masonry to cast them down on defenceless councillors, and he was frightening to behold. His magic had bulged his muscles and bulked out his frame to grotesque proportions, so much so that his deformed magnificence brought back whispers of the giants depicted in the old stories. Her magic had been stronger.

She had pushed him back until they left the town and ascended the mountains beyond, into an alpine environment she rarely visited.

That was when he had lifted a hundred tons of snow and sent it crashing towards her. An airborne avalanche. She hadn't expected that.

She'd had to leave, had to link in to the commonality of all magic and transport herself away, because, mistress of cold and heat or not, melting that much snow at once would have left her defenceless. And if she had done nothing the immense weight would have crushed her. Either way, the Void Worker would have finished her. So she jumped.

The problem with commonality, of course, was that all magic users could access it, and as she jumped, the Void Worker transferred his focus from the avalanche to her leap, his power added to her own sending her far further than she had ever intended to go. Cassie had never been here before. Never been somewhere so bare or inhospitable. So cold.

The wind clung to her, whirling its fingers around her so the furred fibres of her hat glued together in a fragile spider's web of icicles and the tips of her eyelashes became stunning displays of crystalline tears, each jagged prism another corner of beauty. Cassie made sure she directed a little of her power to a current running just beneath her irises, preventing the water that lubricated the surface of her eyes from freezing over. The idea of blindness terrified her.

The balance was hard. To keep her heart, lungs, liver alive, she couldn't let any of the heat escape, had to keep it centralised and internal, and as a result she could feel a pane of ice growing slowly on her cheek, sheening it over like glass until it felt like the skin of a frozen angel. There was no denying that all these budding structures, all these blossoming flowers of crystal water were beautiful, but as someone who could control rivers, make fires dance, and bring an oak from green sapling to royal height and crashing fall in the space of seconds, she knew that just because something was beautiful it didn't mean it was safe.

Had she been almost any other person, she would be dead by now. The blood would have solidified inside her veins within minutes. And she had used an awful lot of her reserves fighting the Void Worker – she didn't dare try to transport herself home. That kind of magic took energy she didn't have, and there was no knowing how far home was from here. If she tried to get home she risked failing, wasting all her power in a vain and dangerous attempt that would leave her crumpled and broken in the snow with nothing to protect her.

Better to keep the magic rationed. Keep on walking.

She hoped that soon she might chance upon some sign of human life – if not actual people, then a dropped tool or the ashes of a dead fire. So far the only life she had seen was animal: a wary white fox here, a sharp-beaked bird fluffed up against the wind there – and two nights ago the fearsome bulk of a great white bear, the stench of rotting seal blubber on his breath and a hunting look in his eye. She had scared him away with a blast of heat that singed the fur of his paws charcoal black, but that was when she had had to start drawing the power from her limbs and limiting it to the most important parts of her body. She hoped she wouldn't see his type again.

By the heavens, it was hopeless out here. As Cassie trudged on through the snow her thoughts drifted to home, images and memories playing across the white page of the icy plain. It was a city. Not a home in the traditional sense, family gathered round the fire, but a spiritual home, one of the greatest accumulations of magical people on the known earth. Magic users flocked there, to this city at the crossroads of the world, to exchange stories and meet other mages, to learn how to control and hone their innate skills until any commoner would pay a handsome fee for the hire of their gifts. There were people there, not one of them a blood relative, who were more family to her than the parents who raised her. People whose hearts sang with the same truths as hers, and knew what it was to have a power running through you that was your whole life, but that could kill you if you pushed too far. There was Boden.

Boden had been one of the last people she had met in the City of Crossroads, but they had in days formed a bond stronger than others formed over years. He was a quiet man, measured, the kind of man who is very good at just sitting and listening, and who took far more from your words than you could ever know. His gift was Mind Magic. When he listened, it wasn't just vocal tones he picked up, but the lilt of your thoughts and the taste of your emotions. And, if you let him, he could walk the avenues of your mind like another man through a garden, knowing exactly what it was you wanted to let him know, and perhaps a few things you didn't. There were people that said his was the most dangerous magic of all.

Walking along, the snow creaking beneath her boots, Cassie closed her eyes and concentrated, focusing her thoughts on one person, one place. Hoping against hope that the distance was not too much, that their close friendship would enable her to be heard, Cassie threw her mind towards Boden. Praying.

Boden?

Yes, Cassie? I'm here.

I'm lost. Far, far from home. It's cold. I might die.

You won't die, Cassie. Stay calm. You're strong. I will find you.

I don't know that you'll be quick enough.

She listened, waiting for the next reply, but none came. There was no answering thought to comfort her, no deep male voice echoing around in the chambers of her skull. Just the roar of wind across ice.

The tears froze on her cheeks. Cassie, heart breaking with the fear of a lonely death, opened her eyes.

She would carry on walking. She would carry on, each moment searching for a house, a splash of green. She would search for life, so that she might keep hers. And maybe, in his silence, Boden could find a way to get to her, and take her home.

Reaching up to peel the sheet of ice away from the raw skin of her cheek, Cassie took another step forward.

About the author: Sarah Cuming has just finished a Masters in Writing at the University of Warwick and is eagerly awaiting her mark. She has had a few short stories published and is currently working on a novel. Check her out on Twitter: @Sarah_Cuming

The Truest Black by Celia Coyne

As night fell upon the house the flowers began to release their strong, spicy perfume; a heady combination of cinnamon and musk. Frank had placed them in a large jam jar and their tall stems splayed untidily over the mantelpiece. In the fading light the tangle of stems and fleshy leaves had taken on the form of a giant, leggy spider.

Gradually, in gentle drifts of air, the scent began to pervade the house. It was carried through the hallway and up the stairs until it reached the back bedroom where Frank lay asleep. He began to dream, his thoughts flitting back through the day's events to the point where he had come across the flowers.

His first reaction had been surprise because of the way the seven long stems were just lying there on the occasional table next to his sofa. He wondered who had put them there and when.

The blooms were a deep velvet black, each with five fleshy petals that fanned out to form a star. The very edges of the petals were silver, as if someone had delicately dipped them in metallic paint. Frank didn't know much about flowers or plants, but he thought they were pretty impressive. They reminded him of the hot-house orchids Mrs Jones liked to cultivate and show at the annual village fete. It occurred to him that maybe Mrs Jones had left the flowers there. His back door was always open and perhaps she had popped round while he was out. But she had left them out of water, which was strange. Even Frank knew that cut flowers should be put in water.

The next morning when Frank awoke, he felt as though he had slept deeply. Dangling his legs over the edge of the bed he felt for his slippers with his feet. Then, like he always did, he wrapped himself in his dressing gown and reached for his glasses. There was nothing different from his usual morning ritual until he went to clean his teeth.

When Frank opened the bathroom door he had quite a shock. Where his avocado suite should have been was the Universe in all its splendour. He quickly shut the door. He had to be dreaming, so he pinched himself and slapped his face – he would have splashed it with water, but he couldn't get into the bathroom, so he slapped his face again. Then he creaked the bathroom door open a fraction. It was still there – stars, galaxies, supernovae, all twinkling in a sea of blackness that went on forever.

He couldn't take it in. *Perhaps this is what psychologists mean when they say someone is having an 'episode'*, he thought. He'd seen a TV programme once, where a psychologist had said that mad people sometimes hallucinated visions, sounds and even smells. *Could it be I've lost my mind?* But Frank didn't feel mad. *Do mad people know they are mad?*

He decided to make himself a cup of tea with two sugars and look again. And sure enough the Universe had not moved. It was mind-blowing; so beautiful and the deepest, truest black he'd ever seen. As he grew more used to it, he let himself hang from the doorframe into the void. He was just beginning to enjoy the unusual sensation of emptiness when his glasses slipped off and away into the black.

Quickly he heaved himself back and shut the bathroom door. *This is dangerous*, he thought, *now my glasses are gone*. He wondered what he should do and then remembered his complete set of *Encyclopaedia Britannica* in the downstairs sitting room. Everything was a blur without his glasses, but he made his way down to the sitting room and managed to find the volume containing 'universe'. Sitting down on the sofa he opened the book on his knees and began to peer closely at the pages. That was when he noticed his glasses. There they were, plain as day, on the occasional table next to the sofa. Thumping the encyclopaedia down, he picked them up. They were definitely his glasses – the very same ones that had slipped off his nose and into space – and perfect, not a scratch on them.

Now something turned in Frank's mind. *Could there be a wormhole in my house?* He had heard about wormholes on science programmes. They were like doorways through space and time. The scientists hadn't said anything about them being dangerous. He decided to experiment.

Taking one of his slippers he ran upstairs and opened the bathroom door. The Universe was still there, quietly infinite. He hurled in the slipper and ran downstairs. Sure enough the slipper materialised right where his glasses had been. *This is amazing*, he thought.

After that Frank threw all sorts of objects into his wormhole: books, a tennis ball, a loaf of bread (which came back perfectly fresh), and a tin of baked beans. He used an egg timer to measure how long it took the items to materialise. Three minutes. He examined every object – but there was never any sign of damage. He spent hours throwing objects into the wormhole until his growling stomach reminded him of the time. It was ten to four – and Mrs Jones, who always popped over on Sundays for afternoon tea, was due to arrive at any moment. Quickly Frank pulled on some clothes and by the time the kettle boiled, Mrs Jones was at the door.

He showed her into the sitting room. The flowers were still in their makeshift vase, and Frank decided he would not mention them; he would wait and see what Mrs Jones had to say. It was then that the idea to put himself through the wormhole came to him. *Can't wait to see the look on her face when I materialise right in front of her!*

Taking the tea tray through from the kitchen, he put it down beside Mrs Jones.

'Help yourself to tea. I'll be three minutes.'

Mrs Jones let the tea brew; she liked it strong. Her visits to Frank were a favour to her friend Maureen, Frank's mum. She glanced around the room; it looked tidy enough, the lad was keeping on top of things. Then her gaze fell upon the strange flowers in the jam jar. They were very unusual. She had always thought a truly black flower was impossible. There was the black parrot tulip, of course, but that was actually a very deep purple. These large, luscious blooms were something else entirely. Blacker than night, blacker than a raven's wing. She stood up to take a closer look. Long, fat stamens were protruding from the flowers. The petals looked so soft and velvety that Mrs Jones felt compelled to touch them. As she did so the flowers scattered a fine dust of silver pollen, like glitter, over the mantelpiece.

Mrs Jones waited for half an hour before she went upstairs to check on Frank. She knocked on the bathroom door before entering – but he was not in there. The house was empty.

'How rude,' muttered Mrs Jones. 'Maureen will have to hear about this. Wandering off like that – it's just bad manners.'

She went back into the sitting room to collect her bag. The pungent odour of the flowers hit her nostrils with a zing and she sneezed, sending the silvery dust everywhere.

When Frank materialised in his front room he was surprised to find it empty. The tea tray was not there and there was no sign of Mrs Jones. He didn't notice it then, but there were no flowers on the mantelpiece either. Frank called through the silent house. There was no one around. Outside the sky was a luminous shade of purple. Suddenly there came a heavy thumping on the front door. Frank hesitated before answering it – he had a feeling that it wouldn't be Mrs Jones…

About the author: Celia Coyne has worked in publishing for 20 years, as a journalist and editor. In her fiction writing she enjoys exploring unusual themes and ideas. She lives in Christchurch, where she is preparing a collection of short stories. Two of her stories have been accepted by New Zealand-based *Takahe* magazine.

Rebirth by Stuart Aken

Centuries had passed since Jared had seen her. Like him at the time, Adelita had been in her prime; a reward for the few remaining males. But Jared had seen her as more than mere recompense for his ability to exist when most of his gender had declined and died. He had always felt more than mere physical desire for her. Something he could not name, though he was sure a name existed for it, somewhere in the distant past. At the time, he'd been sure she had wanted only his genetic rarity. Yet, here she was again, real as ever; her utter perfection mashing his emotions and rippling his deteriorating skin with small tremors.

Zareen, her most recent sisterclone and a close visual, if artificial physical copy, glanced across the soft sterility of his ward at her creator and complained to Jared, 'Adelita's human skin is still soft as a baby's, unlined as a ripening peach. It's just not right. She's organic. How can it be, my Lord?' She shrugged in an attempt to mimic frustration but the bounce of her flawless breasts somehow mocked the act, reducing it to pantomime.

How Zareen could possibly know about babies or peaches was a mystery. Under the recent extension of human rights to premier androids, she was permitted certain memories from her originator. Such a relaxation in the laws had been inevitable almost since the inception of the Preservation Programme, though only of late had clones gained some rights that had been exclusively human. But the last proper baby had yelled her birthing protests over two hundred years before Zareen's incubation. And aromatically enhanced holograms might be impressive but they were a poor substitute for real peaches, if his memory served him well. You couldn't actually touch them, and nothing virtual had the same qualities as reality.

'So, how do you know, Zareen?'

'Imagination. I requested that quality during my first enhancement, my Lord.'

Well, imagination was fine. Reality was what worried Jared. And seeing the reality of that walking epitome of idealised femininity enter his sheltered empire was shock enough to shoot his health indicators way outside their safety zones: conditions his dedicated carers were eager to prevent.

'You wish me to deal with the intruder, Sire?'

Jared allowed the android medics to regain control over his natural functions and felt the air flow smoothly once more through his pipes, the blood cycle as it should around his aged body.

'No. Treat her as the Utmost Celebrity she truly is.'

But he wished her elsewhere; anywhere but close to his bed, where he lay deteriorating as he finally suffered the physical effects of extreme old age. Suppose she recognised him through his decay? All those centuries ago, they'd matched in quality of appearance, intellect, knowledge and, most of all, energy. What was it she'd said, that last time?

'A performance worthy of the occasion, Jared. Emotional component deeply moving, physicality supreme, sensory elements comprehensively targeted and achieved.'

She'd hinted then, through her laughter at her own silliness, at future visits. 'Once I've swum the pool and served the remaining men. Sometime in the not too distant, if that meets with your approval?'

Approval? He'd have had her the next day, and the next and the day after that, ad infinitum. But he hadn't wanted to appear desperate; a man of his standing could have any companion he desired, after all. He never had forgotten her, though.

Now she'd come back. For him? He looked around the ward; his ward, his domain. There was no one else; only the carers and Zareen. With over two thousand commercial sisterclones, Adelita was unlikely to have travelled the Many Ways just to visit an artificial clone that bore her genes. So, was it true?

The male, less robust than the female, had deteriorated much more rapidly than predicted: early research failing to isolate actual problems from the hypothetical and the theoretical. The apparent distance of the threat had allowed energy and research to concentrate on those aspects that ultimately turned out to be favourable mostly to the female. When they'd predicted, millennia previously, the gradual decay of the Y chromosome, they hadn't realised what effect that decline might have on the rest of the male coding.

Oh, sure, Jared was still extant, still a reality. Unlike his fellows; long since reduced to memories and emotions wrapped in the plastaderm of their physically perfect cloned artificials. No longer truly human but, at least, surviving.

But no android, however well constructed, housed Jared's essence and archive. He stubbornly resided in the very body that had struggled down the birthing canal of his mother.

'Natural childbirth? I mean, really? My Lord.' Zareen gently stroked him in apology for her almost lapse. She knew the answer but it was her way of simulating amazement.

Over the centuries, in spite of continual exposure, he'd never come to terms with the eavesdropping ability of Premier Class Sisterclones. That weird skill in attracting, sifting and decoding the brainwaves of those nearby so they could read their thoughts. It was expected between androids but not between android and human. The ability had arisen out of the commercial and biological desire to have sisterclones respond at once to every whim of those few real men who existed at the time. But it had always unnerved Jared.

'Nothing artificial about me, Zareen.' Redundant information and, given the nature of what kept him alive, no longer strictly true. But she'd always found it difficult to accept. Such acknowledgement making her own state somehow less desirable, lower grade than the truly human.

'That's why I still want you, Jared.' Adelita had approached without him noticing.

Close up, she was even more perfect than he recalled; though he knew the phrase broke rules and he'd never dream of saying it aloud.

'Perfect is an absolute and therefore incapable of modification.'

He'd forgotten Adelita's human, and therefore uncanny, ability to read his mind; a by-product of her generous sharing of emotion and skill with her sisterclones, an unexpected consequence of the transfers she'd made with Premiers, like Zareen.

'But I'll forgive the grammatical fault. And even the deterioration of age, repulsive as it is, finds no blame in me. You're still fully functioning, I take it?'

'No idea, Adelita. I haven't "functioned" for a hundred years or more. No need with medics to take the drudgery out of the continued demands made of me.'

'Drudgery, Jared?'

'Artificial insemination. Not the real thing, like it was with you, Adelita. And it was never drudgery with you. Far from it. I was new and freshly made. Energy came naturally. I travelled with you. We made tracks together, found our mutual destination almost at the same instant. But you're not changed one iota. Look at me. You said yourself I've aged, become repulsive. You really can't expect the same of me so many centuries on.'

'I can. And I do.' She displayed a small green vial for him, secreted in her perfect hand, liquid contents swirling with an iridescent glow and the independent movement of a living medium that sent shudders through his fragile frame.

He'd heard about this. Never seen it. Always thought it an untruth put about by Them. Make a promise like that and They knew he'd cling on in hope, no matter what. And he had clung on. Taken every step to keep existence actual. Avoided the final, ultimate artificial cloning.

'It's real enough.'

He felt rather than heard her truth and knew it to be so. By space, she was something to see; always had been. And the scent of her. So much female pheromone in one enduringly lovely package.

They were close in many ways; like him, she'd been a foetus.

'Is it true, My Lord? You both were children of nature, infants...actually suckling at your mothers'...breasts, My Lady?' Zareen quivered.

'Only recent custom and utilitarian tradition have made the images in your mind obscene, Sisterclone. There was much soft and natural about it, then.'

'Yes. It's true, Zareen. We knew our mothers. Sucked milk and life where now only sensation lives.'

Adelita glanced sympathy at Zareen and passed a well-known secret to Jared. 'Artificial has no true understanding of Natural; the reality of it disappears with processing. That's why you and I must be and continue.'

It amazed him that she transmitted as easily as she received. Was that also a gift of the phial?

'Partly, yes.' She presented it again. 'Will you?'

The gift promised but the threat made him tremble. 'I've heard it pains more than one can possibly imagine.'

She nodded.

'You?'

Again, that perfect face, framed by wavy pale gold, slowly rose and fell. It was then he saw beyond the intensity of those aquamarine eyes that flashed her want of him. In the depths of her pupils, the pain she'd felt and held echoed within her. The price.

'The pain has gone now?'

'Almost.'

'And you were really once as...?'

'Yes. Even more repulsive, if that's possible. But age was ever more cruel to women than men. There's a dignity to age in males that finds only pathos and fear of rejection in females.'

It was impossible to picture her in skin as old and dry as his. The bent bones, blackened teeth, slow aching joints, the hirsute sprouting regalia of age.

She smiled. 'An accurate portrayal. But reversible, as you see. Will you?'

'How long in agony?'

'A week at least; maybe up to a year.'

'Afterwards?'

'Echoes. Memories. Mutual bliss will cover the residues.'

He finally understood 'why'. She needed him to give her peace. Artificial clones were expert technicians but lacked the true warmth of the human. No matter how engineers might perfect robotics, machines were still machines, even when they housed the memories and feelings of the real men and women they mimicked.

He was human still. And she was supreme amongst living women. And she wanted him.

'Take it.' The phial lingered in her palm, offered.

'Why haven't They provided it, if it does all you say?'

She nodded, acknowledging his scepticism. 'They believe the risk is too high. Having made Their promises and provided this, They now consider the risk of actual use too high a price to pay. It was ever the way with Them, as you know, Jared.'

'And that risk is?'

She sat then, on the edge of the floating anti-grav that gave him soft support without pressure. 'There's a small chance you might die.'

He looked into her eyes and knew she told the truth but wondered at her definition of small.

'Less than one in twenty. And I demonstrate the risk is worth it. Will you defy Them and take the chance, before they come to destroy the only remaining phial?'

She held it up for his examination again and he watched the swirling threat and promise move within the small glass tube.

'They say it both restores and preserves. Does it?'

'Would I risk it otherwise? Risk you? It has restored me from the state I was; a state worse than your current condition. This is the last. I brought it for you because you are the one I want. There's only Jared. Only one. No more. The last.'

Surprising that she said it with such conviction.

'Am I?'

Amongst the many billions, how could she be sure?

'I know. Even without official records, even without the Universal Brain, which agrees with me, there are signs if you search. And you know how thorough I can be.'

It was true, he knew. He found a memory of his time with her to curve his mouth. Saw it reflected in her face.

'Will you, Jared? For me.'

'How long will it give us?'

'I've already had an extra century, which I've spent in vainly searching for other men. There are none. Just you, Jared. And, even if there had been, I would eventually have been forced to come for you; to spend the rest of time with.'

'The rest of time? As short as that?'

She allowed a small smile and held the phial toward him. 'They claim eternity. A millennium or more with you will do for me.'

There was no sign of aging in her. Twenty two or three in terms of what the years once meant, according to the holographic records and his personal memories. And they'd never age.

She held his hand. 'They say that if decline begins after this, it ends the same moment. Live young and strong and vital. Die in an instant of imploding cells.'

'So, we'd end completely, denied the chance of transfer to an artificial clone?'

'After what we have as humans, Jared, after what we will have; who'd settle for a half existence?'

Zareen turned away; the pain of exclusion enough even for her artificial being.

He reached for the phial. Trembling, took it. And, suddenly, he knew the ancient name of what it was he felt for her.

'Yes. I love you, too, Jared. Here, let me.'

Almost as soon as Adelita administered it, he felt the energy course through him.

And, slowly, came the pain.

About the author: Stuart is a prolific writer of science fiction and fantasy and his latest epic trilogy, A Seared Sky, is available now.

About the author, by the author: Born, against the odds, to a widowed artist, in a neighbour's bed. Husband, father, novelist, short story wrangler, agnostic, romantic open-minded radical liberal, sometimes dangerous to know. Find me, and my writing, the only place I ever lie and which, after love, remains my raison dêtre, at stuartaken.blogspot.co.uk

THE

END

FUSION

Thank you dear reader, we hope you enjoyed this anthology and will look out for more from Fantastic Books Publishing.

Follow us on Facebook;
www.facebook.com/FantasticBooksPublishing

Send us a Tweet;
@Fantastic_Books

Go visit our Website;
www.fantasticbookspublishing.com

Any questions? Don't hesitate to contact us;
fantasticbookspublishing@gmail.com

FUSION

FUSION

Made in the USA
Charleston, SC
13 November 2014